OKOYE

TO THE PEOPLE

OKOYE
TO THE PEOPLE

IBI ZOBOI

Los Angeles   New York

First Edition, March 2022

10 9 8 7 6 5 4 3 2 1

FAC-021131-21232

Printed in the United States of America

This book is set in MrsEaves
Designed by Catalina Castro

Library of Congress Cataloging-in-Publication Number: 2021944129

ISBN 978-1-368-04697-8

Reinforced binding

Visit www.DisneyBooks.com
and www.Marvel.com

For the people of Haiti, Bushwick,
Brownsville, and Flatbush

And that's where the whole trouble is. . . . We're too much alike to understand each other because we don't even understand our own selves.

—Betty Smith, *A Tree Grows in Brooklyn*

Spread love, it's the Brooklyn way.

—Notorious B.I.G.

CHAPTER 1

The orange-yellow sun rises over Wakanda and casts a light so bright that Okoye's eyes instantly open. She sits up on her bed eager to sprint through sun rays, morning dew, and tall grass to get to the Upanga Training Facility. But her mandatory morning routine forces her to slow down for quiet reflection, and for gratitude to the ancestors that she is now part of a respected group of some of the bravest women in the world: the Dora Milaje.

Just a few years ago, Okoye was a village girl who would race other children through the bushes, over the hills, and down to the market, where the aunties would sell their harvest and trinkets beneath thatched-roof stalls. From time to time, King T'Chaka would bless the villagers and market people with his presence. The Dora Milaje would walk by his side as they looked sternly out into the distance, where the green mountain ranges touched the long stretch of ocean-blue sky. They would secretly wink or smile at a girl who might soon join their ranks.

This was how it started for Okoye. The day her youthful, impressionable eyes met one of those beautiful, strong, and powerful women, she knew this would be her life. Months of training during which she was broken down to only a relic of her girlish self and built back up to a mighty, wise, and loyal woman, warrior, and protector of Wakanda and its throne have led to this moment when she proudly slips into her Dora Milaje uniform.

Her red tunic and fitted pants are made from a material so tough and light that they feel like a second skin. So she wears the duties of the Dora Milaje on her body and carries them in her heart. The matching armband and boots are an added touch that make her feel that much more powerful. Her spear is not just a weapon—it's become part of her body, like another limb. It folds into the sleeve of her tunic, hidden from plain sight. Okoye slicks some oil over her bald scalp, where the new tattoo has marked her for life, and perhaps, the afterlife.

Ayo is waiting outside her compound, just as eager as Okoye is, even if she isn't smiling. Her clean-shaven head glistens in the morning sunlight and her deep brown skin seems to be covered in starlight. Okoye knows that Ayo is her reflection in every way. She is proud to be a warrior woman alongside her best friend.

There are several compounds at the edge of the forest where the Dora Milaje have made their homes. Each compound is a rounded-edged square structure with white stucco walls, red steel doors, and one-way reflective windows. Hausa symbols are painted around the edges of the doors—secret affirmations each Dora Milaje has to memorize. Many of the Dora have already left their compounds while another group rests after having completed their nightly shifts in the palace. Okoye and Ayo are summoned to the Upanga Training Facility for today, away from their usual duties of guarding the Wakandan throne.

Ayo stops just as the dirt road leading out of the forest opens up to a paved footpath. She holds her spear as a deceptive smile spreads across her face. "How about a little morning exercise before we walk to Upanga?" she asks.

"Shouldn't we wait to see what the captain has in store for us?" asks Okoye.

"A little friendly combat will not hurt," Ayo says, pounding her spear on the ground. "Besides, we will be that much more prepared. It'll be a warm-up. I promise."

Okoye has already unfolded her spear from out of her tunic's sleeve and is in her combat position—her knees bent with one leg forward and one leg back, her right arm extended over her head, ready to knock Ayo's spear out of her hand. Within seconds, the warrior women are dodging each other's weapons as they spin on their heels, kick, swing, and leap. Okoye's movements are swift and fiery while Ayo is steady and patient before she attacks. Okoye quickly twists to deliver a strong jab, but Ayo aims for her legs, and in an instant, Okoye is on the ground, on her back, defeated. But it's only a few seconds before she swings her arm around Ayo's arm at the elbow, weakening her grip on the spear. With all the strength she can muster, Okoye pushes herself up with her legs, taking Ayo's whole body with her. Ayo leaps out of Okoye's grip, and the two women are a few feet away from each other once again, in their combat positions.

A small crowd of children has gathered around them, cheering for their favorite. Half of them are singing Okoye's name, while the others root for Ayo.

Okoye is the first to smile. Ayo relaxes her body. The children applaud, and most of them return to their chores or long walks to school. About five girls stay back, looking up at Okoye and Ayo in awe.

"When we are older, we want to be just like you!" a girl says.

Another girl motions with her arm as if to release a folded spear. She swings her imaginary weapon at the other girl, and they are in battle while speaking an unintelligible gibberish that is supposed to be Hausa.

Okoye and Ayo laugh. "Soon, my young sisters," Okoye says. "Soon."

"Make sure Mistress Zola takes notice of you when you demonstrate your skills," Ayo adds.

The girls disperse, running, laughing, and swapping dreams of how they will one day protect Wakanda as Okoye and Ayo head to the Upanga Training Facility. Ayo is moving slower than before.

"What is the matter?" Okoye asks. "Are you hurt?"

"Hurt? Me? Never," Ayo says. "You, on the other hand, must be tired. You were breathing hard, my sister."

"Tired? Me? Never," Okoye says, standing straight and folding her spear back into her sleeve. "We can fight all day, if you want. But Captain Aneka would

reprimand us for practicing when we have more important matters to tend to."

"You are correct. After all, you need your rest."

"And you need to tend to your sore muscles."

This small moment of joy and playfulness between
the two warrior women slowly wears off as the morning
sun inches toward the middle of the sky.

"You know," Okoye says, "we mustn't be so careless
around the villagers. They must see us as noble and
disciplined at all times."

"I disagree. They must see us as humans and not as
warrior robots created in one of Wakanda's many technological labs."

"You are correct," Okoye concedes. "After all, those
village girls were looking up to us. I suppose they
want to see the possibility of what they can achieve in
Wakanda. They can be artisans if they want. They can
be healers or have their own businesses."

"They can be poets or spies; seamstresses or carpen-
ters," says Ayo.

"Physicists or singers; botanists or chemists," Okoye
adds. "Don't you see how prodigious little Shuri has
become? The princess is sure to create an entirely new
universe in that play lab of hers."

"Yes, that one is just a ball of raw talent and potential.

And of course, any girl in Wakanda can become a Dora Milaje."

"If they succeed at passing all the trials. Don't you think Captain Aneka will become much stricter as time goes on?" Okoye asks.

"Wakanda may change during our time as Dora Milaje," Ayo says. "I've been out there in the world and I've seen how nations have fallen and risen. We may need to shift our skills as times change."

"Do you think this is what the meeting with Captain Aneka is all about?"

"I do not know. But in any case, we have both gotten a little workout from our battle this morning. I am ready for whatever assignment will come our way."

"I am not sure, Ayo," Okoye says, lowering her voice. "I am just getting used to guarding the king and getting to know the royal family. I don't think I want to be sent off to a new assignment just like you were a couple of months ago."

"I understand, my sister. I, too, was barely a new Dora Milaje when I accompanied Captain Aneka on my first trip outside Wakanda. But being whisked away to new adventures at a moment's notice is all part of our calling. Accept it with grace, Okoye. Village girls are looking up to you. You are a role model now."

"A role model? Me? A whole me?" Okoye jokes with a smile.

"Yes, my sister. A whole you. Okoye of Wakanda and the mighty and brave Dora Milaje," Ayo says.

The two women laugh as they make their way to the Upanga Training Facility. But as soon as passersby come close, they shift into their serious Dora Milaje stances— face forward, shoulders back, alert, tall, and regal.

CHAPTER 2

The warm morning breeze grazes the tops of Okoye's and Ayo's heads, and their tattoos shimmer in the sunlight. Just a few seasons ago, they had dreams of protecting King T'Chaka and Wakanda as warrior women of the Dora Milaje. Those girlhood wishes are now their reality. Okoye's chest puffs out with pride as they make their way to Upanga. But they must stay grounded and centered, exuding a commanding presence, even if they are still like buoyant, giggling village girls on the inside.

"Ayo, I have certainly gotten much stronger since becoming a Dora Milaje," Okoye says. "I am swifter and lighter on my feet. I almost feel invincible."

"Ah, Okoye. Captain Aneka taught us that strength is not only physical. It is mental and—"

"Spiritual," Okoye adds. "I know, I know. But when we fight, it is with our bodies and strong muscles, yes? Our strength as the people of Wakanda is not from magic but muscles and brain power, am I correct?"

"Our ancestors guide us, too," Ayo says.

"In the middle of battle when we call on the Black Panther, he doesn't descend from the clouds hanging over Wakanda. It is the science of the Kimoyo beads that brings him to us."

"Do you not remember what Captain Aneka has told us? As Dora Milaje women and warriors, we can be all things at once: spirit, science, and pure strength."

"Ah, yes. Like the sun, moon, and stars. They all exist in the sky," Okoye says. "Then we are like the sky."

"And like the earth with its mountains, valleys, oceans, and rivers," Ayo adds. "We are like Wakanda."

"Ha! I like that. We are Wakanda!" Okoye says.

Then they turn to each other and say, "Forever!"

Upanga's arched roof and tinted windows become visible in the distance, past the trees and flower bushes lining the paved road leading to its elaborate red double doors where two spears cross each other. As soon as Okoye and Ayo step onto the mat where the words *Dora*

Milaje are inscribed in gold, the doors open up to the wide and majestic rotunda of the training facility.

In the center of the brightly lit rotunda, standing over a Black Panther insignia, is Captain Aneka, wearing her white-and-gold tunic and matching pants. Her hands are clasped in front of her and her short, cropped hair glistens under the lights. "Good morning, warriors!" she says in Hausa, one of the languages of Wakanda, with only a hint of a smile. "I am so elated to see you."

"Good to see you again, Captain," Ayo says. "We will only be elated once we know what this is all about."

"Well, I am elated to see you, Captain," Okoye says, bowing her head out of respect.

"Ha! Ayo is right. Hold your enthusiasm, Okoye. Tell me, how have you been?"

"We are doing well," Okoye says.

"We are better than well," says Ayo. "Did you expect otherwise, Captain?"

"Of course not. This is why one of you has been chosen for this special assignment."

Okoye and Ayo quickly exchange glances. Captain Aneka had sent a message via a Kimoyo bead for Okoye and Ayo to meet her first thing in the morning in Upanga. Excitement had stirred in Okoye's belly, but she's learned to keep her emotions at bay. When duty calls, she mustn't revert to her girlish fantasies of action and adventure. On the day she received her noble and very important assignment to be a guard for King T'Chaka alongside Aneka, she wanted to leap toward the sky with joy. But she's learned to maintain a stern and controlled presence, even when her emotions are like a turbulent river.

On most days, Okoye and Ayo stand beside the king as he meets with the Tribal Council, during his briefings with intertribal representatives, and when he's addressing his son, Prince T'Challa. This is when it's harder for Okoye to keep a stern face. She can still recall T'Challa playing along the grassy edges of the palace wall as a little boy. Now he is busy with his own combat trainings and trying to impress his father. Little Shuri makes her presence known from time to time, poking fun at Okoye's bald head and stoic facade. Okoye has mastered the art of suppressing her laughter, thank goodness.

Captain Aneka paces up and down around them, her boots clicking against the marble floor of the rotunda. The captain stops just a few feet in front of Okoye. Her face is stern, but her eyes are smiling, letting Okoye and Ayo know that while she is strict, she cares deeply about the Dora Milaje.

"You may be wondering why I called you here this morning," the captain says. "Firstly, I apologize for pulling you away from your duties. I've sent two other Dora Milaje as substitutes. The king understands. However, one of you, the noble women of the Dora Milaje, has been presented with a tremendous opportunity. Ayo, since you have already been on this special mission, I have invited you here to support your warrior sister Okoye."

Okoye feels her insides leap, but she is as still as a baobab tree. She glances over at Ayo, checking for any sign of excitement on her face. Ayo quickly winks at her, so Okoye smiles back only a little—a secret exchange between the two young women expressing anxiety or excitement. Only a few times during their training would they read genuine fear in each other's eyes. But they are long past those days of having to perform strenuous feats and competitive games to demonstrate skill, speed, and strength to be worthy of the Dora Milaje title.

Okoye hangs on to Captain Aneka's every word as she looks at the women with her piercing eyes, scanning each of their faces. Okoye looks at Captain Aneka in admiration. She's always believed her to be a pillar of grace and strength—a stealthy warrior and a master at combat techniques from all around the world.

Aneka is closer to their age, so her achievements seem attainable. Surely, there is more to learn from her, but Okoye has passed all her tests, performed exceedingly well in all the games, and she is now a pillar of grace and strength as well. Okoye's mind races, wondering what this opportunity could be.

"As you already know, the world is much, much larger than Wakanda," Captain Aneka continues. "There are nations and cultures, people and places that have their own histories and keep their own secrets."

Okoye raises her hand, and Aneka nods for her to speak up. "Do these other places have anything like Vibranium?"

"Of course not," Captain Aneka snaps. "Vibranium belongs only to Wakanda, just like the Dora Milaje. You are one of a kind: diamonds in a sea of coal, a constellation in the night sky, a rainbow after a storm—"

"We get it, Captain," Ayo interrupts. "We are special."

Okoye tries to hold back a chuckle, but within seconds she is an avalanche of laughter. Soon after, Ayo bursts open with joy.

"Attention!" Captain Aneka shouts in Hausa, and the women immediately stop and stand straight with their arms at their sides, their faces like stone again. "I will not fault you for finding a bit of respite from your new duties. In fact, some laughter here and there—some light conversation and small talk, as they say—will prepare you for this sort of assignment."

Okoye's ears perk up. Ayo smiles a little. It's true. The Dora Milaje are not about warfare and stone faces all the time. Joy slips in like beams of sunlight every now and then, lifting their spirits and lighting their hearts, very much like this morning. Their jobs are not easy, and they are humans, not machines. So laughter is rest. Moments of levity heal wounds from wars not yet fought. Okoye turns to Ayo again, and they exchange genuine smiles this time.

"However, I will need to prepare you for this task, Okoye," the captain says. "And *you* will need to demonstrate to me what you can bring to this assignment. You will be accompanying me to America, where King T'Chaka will be an invited guest. You and I will be his guards. However, we have to tone it down. No Dora Milaje uniform. We can bring our spears, but they must remain discreet and be used only when absolutely necessary."

"I am ready, Captain," Okoye says, trying to contain her excitement.

"She was born ready," Ayo adds, smiling at her friend.

"Very well, then. Follow me."

Okoye and Ayo walk into a small room where a series of strange outfits float in midair, hanging from invisible wires. There are ball gowns and exercise clothes, T-shirts and jeans, sneakers in all colors, and even swimsuits that are a far cry from their Dora Milaje uniforms, which cover every inch of their bodies. A blazer, a fitted skirt, and a pair of heels hover before them as if being worn by a model, but there is no one there. "What is this?" Okoye asks.

"It's business attire," Ayo says.

"I mean, I know what it is. But why is it here?"

"Why don't you try them on for size?" the captain asks. "We already know they fit, but you should learn to be comfortable in this clothing."

Soon Okoye is out of her uniform and into a black blazer, pencil skirt, and black heels. "Who am I supposed to be?" she says.

"A college student. A supermodel. An intern at the Wakandan palace," Aneka says.

"Which one?" Okoye asks.

"All of them. At once! We are going to America, Okoye!" the captain exclaims. "Where you can be all you can be!"

"America!" Okoye squeals, forgetting all her Dora Milaje training to keep her emotions at bay. She can't help it. Joining the ranks of the Dora Milaje is already a dream come true several times over. But traveling to America exceeds everything she could've ever imagined. She quickly composes herself because she will certainly be on duty even outside Wakanda's borders. "This will be very exciting. But we can't be part of an army? Any and everything else but Dora Milaje? I think this will be the hardest part of this assignment, especially wearing those clothes."

"You can wear sneakers with anything in America. You can run, fight, kick in them, and not have to blow your cover," Ayo says as she watches Okoye trying to walk around in the heels. "But I like the heels. Why couldn't we wear something like that when we traveled with the king?"

"Because you were a student then, wide-eyed and oblivious. Now, Okoye, you will be a diplomatic guest. You don't want to blend in too much with the commoners."

Okoye and Ayo exchange smiles. "A guest to whom?" Okoye asks.

Captain Aneka smiles deceptively. "There is more for me to teach you, warrior woman. Let us go," she says.

Okoye soon becomes accustomed to her new outfit, still without knowing the details of this assignment. As her heels click-clack on the marble floors of the facility,

Captain Aneka motions for her and Ayo to follow her into another room.

A small group of other Dora Milaje is seated around a table that is covered with fancy plates, wineglasses, silver cutlery, and elaborate place settings.

"A dinner party? At this time of the morning?" Okoye asks.

Captain Aneka simply pulls out two seats for Okoye and Ayo as the other Dora Milaje politely greet them with slight nods and gentle smiles—odd gestures from their fellow warrior women, who usually exchange a few jovial Hausa words with one another.

Okoye is awkward around the table. Sure, she's been to dinners in the palace where she would stand guard by the door as the king hosts his guests. But the Dora Milaje take turns eating meals out of sight, sometimes while standing outside the servants' quarters where the meals are prepared, and other times late at night after they've fulfilled their duties. Sitting around a table like this is a luxury.

"Don't get too comfortable," the captain says. "Your sister warriors are here to help."

"Do you care to tell us what this is all about?" Ayo asks.

"Formalities," Captain Aneka says as she paces around the table with her hands clasped behind her.

"Niceties and pleasantries. You've all seen in one way or another how our beloved king has entertained his guests—other members of the royal court, tribespeople, and even humble villagers with a special invitation. Except our king is not as shallow as the people you will meet on the other side of Wakanda's borders. Way on the other side, in America."

Okoye's heart leaps as she thinks of all the adventures that await in that foreign country, but she remains calm to receive more details.

"Okoye, observe your sister warriors as they serve themselves while engaging in light conversation. Please remember this: napkin on the lap, salad fork, dinner fork, knife, spoon. Water glass, wineglass. However, in other parts of the world, you are too young to drink. You have a couple more years."

"Ayo tells me that at twenty-one it will be legal for us to drink in America, while at eighteen you can go to war and are expected to kill your enemies," Okoye says as she glances at Ayo, who only gives her a knowing nod. Soon she is mimicking the Dora Milaje's gestures as they serve their meals and ask strange questions about the weather and compliment the unusually bland food that is certainly not part of the traditional Wakandan fare—a far cry from their customary ways of eating out of calabash bowls, sometimes with their bare fingers because mashed yams with a spicy sauce demand it. "I don't understand, Captain," Okoye says. "We are not unfamiliar with American customs. We know how to eat at such tables. Why must we engage in such frivolous activity?"

"This is not about civility. This is about diplomacy," Captain Aneka says as she gracefully cuts her vegetables into tiny bite-sized pieces. "Okoye, we are going to New York City!"

Okoye nearly chokes on a piece of lettuce. "New York City?"

"Yes, the richest city in America. Almost like Wakanda, but it doesn't hide its wealth from the world." Captain Aneka holds out her right hand, where a single Kimoyo bead rests in her palm. The bead projects a light beam that becomes a hologram. Within its iridescent walls, a silhouette of a tree appears with the initialism NNLB. "The king has to make several rounds of diplomatic meetings, and he has been invited by an internationally renowned organization called No Nation Left Behind Industries. They've been pestering our king for some time now and King T'Chaka has finally obliged. A woman by the name of Stella Adams has personally invited the king. He's been told that his help is needed to do some good around the world, and you know our king. If it's a humanitarian mission, then he doesn't need much convincing to leave Wakanda to, at the very least, spread his message of hope and peace."

The hologram shifts into an image of a blond woman with her arms folded across her chest. She smiles a little, but there is something discomforting about her eyes— cold and piercing. Or it may just be how Americans photograph themselves to show the world that they have power and control, even over their own facial expressions. No matter. Okoye only takes in the details of her face for future reference.

"Will he be in any danger?" Okoye asks, glancing at Ayo, who has barely shared anything about her brief time in New York City. "We will protect him at all costs."

"Ayo, have you not instructed your sister warrior on what the world is like outside Wakanda?"

"What's to tell? The first and last time I was in New York City, I simply followed you and the king around like a palace pet," Ayo says in a tone unfamiliar to Okoye.

"Our Royal Highness King T'Chaka likes to make an appearance in the world when he feels it's necessary," Captain Aneka continues. "It's important that we represent Wakanda exactly how the world believes us to be: a humble African nation that is willing to extend its grace to other nations. Nothing more, nothing less."

"Well, that is true, isn't it?" Okoye asks. She picks

up a piece of bread to sop up some gravy—the way she would eat mashed yams and a spicy sauce with her hands—but another Dora Milaje slaps away her hand and motions for her to use a spoon.

"Yes, but there shall be no word of Vibranium or your training as Dora Milaje. We don't want to arouse suspicion as to why a small and humble nation like Wakanda would need powerful female warriors such as ourselves."

"When I went to New York City," Ayo says, "the king introduced me as a student."

"It was not entirely untrue," Captain Aneka says. "You were a Dora Milaje in training. You were certainly a student."

"Then what will be our roles?" Okoye asks.

A deceptive smile spreads across Captain Aneka's face. "You can be whatever you want to be in America. If you can make it in New York City, you can make it anywhere, as they say. But, as for your duties, you are to stay alert at all times, making sure our king is safe. I believe that he will be in good hands as an invited guest. However, I worry that New York City has plenty of petty thieves, or anyone who will want to take advantage of newcomers."

Okoye looks at Ayo with inquisitive eyes and a string of questions swirling around in her head. Petty thieves in a place as wealthy as New York City? Whatever the case, if this is part of her Dora Milaje duties, then she is more than ready and willing. There is no room for questions and doubts. She must answer the call and fulfill her king's wishes with every ounce of her Dora Milaje soul.

CHAPTER 3

"It is just like Wakanda," Captain Aneka says, reassuring Okoye, whose eyes are darting about in the bustling airport. "Except faster and . . . less civilized."

"Hmph," Okoye responds, quickening her pace to keep up with both the captain and King T'Chaka. "*Much less civilized.*" It's been one month since she learned of this trip, and Okoye has spent that time learning as much as she could about New York City. But nothing could prepare her for the bustling energy and the rude people who barely smile.

"We do not want to be disrespectful, however," Aneka says. "No judgment, no ridicule. Just . . . compassion."

"Right, *compassion*," Okoye says, holding her head up higher this time as the passersby bump into her without apologizing, stare at her with wide eyes, or simply ignore her. She's learned to walk quickly in these high-heeled shoes. Her lesson with Captain Aneka and the other Dora Milaje is proving to be quite useful. After a few days of walking around in heels and a skirt in the Upanga Training Facility, she is comfortable enough to run, jump, or drop-kick someone in the face if she needs to, and still appear *professional*.

King T'Chaka is a special envoy to the World Humanitarian Aid Council in New York City. Captain Aneka has accompanied the king to America several times, taking with her newly trained Dora Milaje. Okoye is the lucky one this time, and while she's comfortable with these new professional clothes, she still fidgets with her wig: a flattering bob that feels as if a lazy hyena is sprawled out over her head. Its warm, itchy fur grazes her high cheekbones. Okoye wants nothing more than to yank these stupid things off her—the wig, the suit, everything. But she is on duty. She is Dora Milaje—a highly skilled, lethal warrior. Discipline, sacrifice, and loyalty are embedded in her Wakandan bones. Besides, Captain Aneka is here to keep her in check.

"And you mustn't be so stiff," Aneka says. Her eyes are steady now, keeping watch on both the king and anyone who comes within a few feet of him. "Smile, nod, and be polite."

"Stiff?" says Okoye. "Captain, are we here to protect our king or . . . walk a runway like fashion models?"

"Ah, yes! Fashion models. That wouldn't be so bad. Remember, on our last visit here, we posed as students."

"And you did not correct them? You did not invoke the name of the Dora Milaje?"

"No. Not here. And you shouldn't either."

"Then who *are* we here?"

"I am a fashion model from Wakanda. Who are you?"

Okoye slows her pace just enough to catch the side-eye from Aneka. "Dora Milaje," she mumbles, just as a loud whistle forces her to quickly turn to meet the perpetrator's gaze. Okoye is ready to attack, but the man just winks at her and smiles.

"Welcome to America, sweetheart!" he calls out with a raspy voice.

Okoye shoots him a sharp look and turns away.

"You should say *thank you*," Aneka whispers.

But Okoye ignores her as curbside agents help King T'Chaka with his luggage. Okoye rushes to grab the suitcases from them, but Aneka pulls her arm, stopping her from getting any closer. "It's their job," she says.

"Then are we to simply stand beside our king and look . . . pretty?"

Aneka pulls her in to whisper into her ear. "Okoye,

we are and will always be Dora no matter where we go. Remember when I said we can be anything here? They may call us what they wish. But we know who we are."

Okoye slowly steps away while keeping her eye on the king. "Fine," she mumbles. "Though I'd much rather be a guard than a fashion model. But being a student wouldn't be so bad."

"We can be guards *and* fashion models *and* students. So, sure, if anyone asks, we are both attending university—Wakanda University," Aneka says as she rushes to walk beside her king.

"Wakanda University," Okoye repeats under her breath as she recalls all her friends back in her village who were just starting their classes as she was beginning her training.

King T'Chaka and the two Dora Milaje walk out of the airport side by side, heads held high, with the dignity and strength of all their fellow Wakandans, but with the humility of a small, peaceful African nation come to share its goodwill with the rest of the world. Their first stop will be Midtown Manhattan for several planning meetings and conferences.

But Okoye's heel gets stuck in a crack on the sidewalk just as a strong wind blows off her wig, revealing her clean-shaven head and the signature Dora Milaje tattoo. She doesn't even flinch. She simply removes her foot from the stuck shoe and lets the wig fly off into the cool city breeze.

"It's the will of the ancestors," she whispers as she limps with one bare foot to the black SUV that pulls up to the curb.

It's only when she is sitting in the backseat of the car that Captain Aneka and the king notice her defiance. Aneka glances at her from the passenger's seat while King T'Chaka, who is seated beside her, says, "I understand, Okoye. This will take some getting used to. It will all become clear. But for now, cover up!"

"Yes, my king," Okoye says softly, swallowing hard and smoothing down the back of her bare head.

"We have more," Aneka says without looking back at her. "We have more shoes, clothes, and hair."

An older man jumps into the driver's seat after helping to load the trunk. Okoye examines him closely, but the man only turns back, smiles, and says, "I heard you need shoes, clothes, and hair. You girls must be supermodels. Gorgeous!"

"Yes, *supermodels*," Aneka says.

"And, sir?" he says, turning to the king. "You must be their manager."

"Manager? I am King T'Chaka of Wakanda!"

"Of course you are! That poor little country. I feel sorry for those people over there," the man says, and drives out of the airport and onto the highway headed toward Manhattan.

Okoye forces herself not to gaze out the window like a wide-eyed tourist. She's been trained to survey every passing car and its passengers. She's learned to read the eyes, faces, and bodies of anyone tasked with having the life of the king in their hands. She watches the driver closely, and so does Captain Aneka.

But the passing sky and buildings are seducing Okoye with their gray and brown colors, their straight lines and sharp angles. Being in this place feels as if she's stepped back in time. No one here knows the majesty that Wakanda holds, and no one here could ever know the power that she wields as a new member of the Dora Milaje.

Captain Aneka and the other Dora back home told her that this was a special mission. She has been chosen for this. She has prepared for this. But now that she is here, she is forced to fold her true self into a tight skirt and high heels. This is the hard part, Okoye realizes.

But, as always, anything for her king. Any and everything for Wakanda.

CHAPTER 4

"The Waldorf Astoria!" the driver sings as he pulls up to the magnificent structure. "Fit for kings and queens, or supermodels and their manager."

Okoye inhales deep, annoyed at the driver's igno rance of who she really is—a Dora Milaje, a title she's worked so hard to earn her entire life. "We are students at the university," she says.

"Oh good," the driver says. "I hear modeling careers have an expiration date, so might as well get a degree in something useful."

Okoye shakes her head, ready to correct the driver. But Aneka gently touches her arm to stop her from speaking any further.

"Thank you for your service," Aneka says, slipping

a wad of cash into the driver's hand before sliding out of the passenger seat.

When Okoye steps out onto the bustling streets of Midtown, the driver whistles at her and she turns, knowing that there's nothing she can do except keep a calm, stern face.

"Hey, sweetheart! Where can I find you again? On the cover of *Vogue*? Victoria's Secret fashion show?" He smiles, revealing yellow and crooked teeth.

"Yes!" Aneka quickly answers for Okoye. "On the cover of *Vogue*!"

***

Captain Aneka has brought with her a couple of gowns, some cocktail dresses, a few leggings, sweatpants, T-shirts, and several versions of the same outfit—dark gray and black suits, black heels, and wigs. This is their uniform for now—a far cry from their fitted red warrior tunics and pants. King T'Chaka has meetings and dinners lined up for the evening where he will discuss the glories of Wakanda, a humble, poor African nation whose warmth and hospitality will charm anyone, despite refusing humanitarian aid for itself. Stella Adams had asked him to share stories about his home country. They attend a cocktail party in the large ballroom on the ground floor of the hotel to honor all the special envoys to the humanitarian mission—kings, presidents, prime ministers, and heads of state from all over the world.

"Please, Dora Milaje, don't make yourself strangers to this place," King T'Chaka says. "We will certainly be back to New York. But for now, don't stand so close. Walk around. Mingle. Discuss the weather. Be . . . *diplomatic*."

"As you wish, my king," both Okoye and Aneka say.

And they do as they are told. Aneka is much more graceful than Okoye since she regularly attends these functions with the king. Nonetheless, Okoye has also been trained well to blend into a room like this. Both Okoye and Aneka smile, nod, and laugh at unfunny jokes as a form of diplomacy. Nothing more, nothing less.

Okoye slowly sips from a glass of sparkling water. A tray of hors d'oeuvres passes her, and she grabs a tiny cucumber sandwich and holds it between her fingers. The whole thing is too small and delicate to satisfy her hunger.

Okoye notices a woman watching her out of the corner of her eye. She stays focused on her king, but this woman has her attention, too. The woman sizes up Okoye, swirls the wine in her glass, takes a big gulp, and makes her way over to her.

Okoye only turns to the woman after she's been standing there for a few long seconds.

"Hey, young lady. You look just as awkward as I do," the woman says. Her smile is bright. Her eyes are fixed on Okoye.

"Awkward?" Okoye asks.

"You're either too young to be here or too bored to care about any of this. Or both. And that cucumber sandwich is not it. I'm going for a burger after this," she says, gently taking the cucumber sandwich from Okoye and chucking it into a nearby trash can. "Lucinda Tate." The woman holds her hand out for Okoye to shake. "And no one, absolutely no one, calls me Lucy."

Okoye hesitates, sets her glass down, and glances at T'Chaka, who is busy chatting amid a circle of politicians and businesspeople. It's Aneka who meets her eyes and nods—a gentle affirmation that she should indeed be socializing with this Lucinda Tate.

But Lucinda quickly takes back her hand. "I apologize. Wakanda, right? I have to admit that I don't know all the customs. You don't seem to be the handshake and small-talk type. But I'm a hugger, if that's the Wakandan way."

Then Okoye holds out a stiff hand. Lucinda takes it and gives it a firm shake.

"I get it. You're being diplomatic. Diplomacy is the name of the game here. Smile, nod, shake hands, and once you turn your back, go to war," Lucinda says.

"War? I thought this was an event for humanitarian missions," Okoye says. She is willing to entertain this woman's chatter, but out of the corner of her eye, someone else catches her attention. The entire room seems to take a breath as a tall blond woman glides across the floor and makes a beeline for King T'Chaka. Okoye immediately recognizes her as Stella Adams, the woman she'd seen through the Kimoyo bead, the one who'd invited her king to America. Her cold, piercing eyes are the same. She certainly did not need a photograph to capture her power and control. She exudes it, and everyone appears to be under some sort of spell when she walks past them. It is almost as if this Stella Adams is the queen of this place.

"Yeah, it's all about peace and humanity, all right. But peace comes at a high cost. Be careful of those who are always willing to pay the hefty price," Lucinda says, pointing her chin in the direction of the other woman. "She doesn't waste any time."

"It's a pleasure meeting you, Lucinda Tate. I must attend to my duties now," Okoye says, while keeping her eyes on this new woman, the king, and Aneka.

"Duties? Now what does that king of yours have you doing?"

Okoye doesn't answer. She walks over to Aneka and quietly stands beside her.

"Not too close," Aneka says. "Order from the king. Go back and . . . mingle."

But Okoye watches the tall blond woman as she smiles and chats with King T'Chaka.

"Stella Adams," Okoye asks. "She is the one in control, isn't she?"

"Yes, she is, according to the Kimoyo bead. And she seems to have taken a liking to our king. She's done a lot of good in New York City."

"So she wants King T'Chaka to help, or the other way around? There was a lady who told me to be careful of her."

"Diplomacy means that they help each other. She can be an ally, a new business partner, a special envoy to a neighboring African nation. It's none of our business. There's nothing here to suggest that the king is in danger, Okoye. Now go."

Okoye exhales and steps away from Aneka, walking stiffly around the room. She is unsure of how to be graceful and cordial. Normally, she would be holding her spear at her side, but this is not normal. This is not home in Wakanda. She is not a true Dora Milaje here. This mockery of herself, this masking of her true identity, was not part of her training.

"Here." Lucinda suddenly appears beside Okoye and hands her a glass of red liquid.

Okoye doesn't take the glass from her.

"It's cranberry juice, by the way. I overheard your king saying that you're a student," Lucinda says, She places the full glass on a nearby table and steps closer to Okoye. "I see you staring at the woman. Her name is Stella Adams. Real estate mogul. That one was a freebie. You're welcome."

Okoye turns to face Lucinda. "What do you want?"

Lucinda chuckles. "Look around, sis."

Okoye doesn't budge. She's done nothing but observe everything and everyone at this cocktail party. She may not know their names or what business they have here, but she knows how far or close they are to the king, their body language, their facial expression, and their overall energy. She's observed that Lucinda Tate is well meaning but annoying. "What do you want? Okoye asks again.

"One, two, and three," Lucinda says, pointing to herself, Okoye, and then to Aneka across the room. "We're the only sistas up in here. I'm just trying to help you out, little *sis*. You know, make a connection. You remind me of the some of the college-age kids in my neighborhood."

Okoye watches Lucinda Tate walk away. Yes, there are only three Black women at this party, but it was never Okoye's duty to befriend all the Black people in New York City.

Someone taps a wineglass with a fork, calling everyone to attention. A short balding man walks to the center of the room. Within seconds, Stella Adams joins him—and she's several inches taller than he and clearly several years younger as well. Okoye feels a flash of regret when she realizes that Lucinda didn't have to tell her to be careful of that woman, but she did, even though Okoye already has those suspicions. The fact that Stella is a real estate mogul sticks out in her mind as the woman refuses to take her eyes off King T'Chaka. Captain Aneka said that, according to the Kimoyo bead, she's done a lot of good. But this Lucinda lady has planted a seed of doubt in Okoye's mind.

The short, balding man holds Stella's hand. "My lovely wife and I would like to thank you—all of you— for joining us this evening. Your work in the world is just as valuable as ours here in the city. You are our eyes and ears out there in those other countries. You can see further in your respective nations. You can hear the whispers and rumblings. Therefore, we consider each of you a valuable asset to the growth of No Nation Left Behind Industries. We have invited you all here to spend a week with NNLB and see what good we are doing in our city. And with your blessings, we hope to expand this good into your respective countries." He raises his glass and a wide smile spreads across his face, making the hairs in his mustache and beard stand at attention. "Here's to uplifting humanity and saving the world, one nation at a time!"

Everyone raises a glass, including Captain Aneka and the king. By the time Okoye finds her glass of cranberry juice on a nearby table, the toast is already done.

As the party continues, Stella leaves her husband to return to her conversation with King T'Chaka.

Okoye steps close to Aneka and asks, "What do you think she wants with the king?"

Aneka sighs. "It's business, Okoye. Business. Or networking, as they say. Can't you see the king is smiling and having a good time? This is a vacation for him. Don't ruin it."

But this is what Okoye trained for. There is something about that blond woman that shifts the air in the room. Her husband has power as the head of No Nation Left Behind Industries, but it is his wife who commands attention. It's as if this Stella Adams is holding the puppet strings to this whole performance. Okoye feels it in her bones.

The guests are sipping their last glasses of wine and

ny colonizers," Okoye says, unim-

," King T'Chaka says. "But it is the

nd a few turns, Brooklyn's landscape
ums and rows of stately brownstones
link of their eyes, some of the build-
nd storefronts look as if they've been
bed. Broken and missing windows
ores and homes. Piles of black trash
the corners of sidewalks. Sirens—
ho above the sparse treetops along

r colonizers here, don't you think?"
ng over at Okoye.
Brooklyn?" King T'Chaka asks.
ly pulls out a Kimoyo bead from her
it in her palm as a hologram of a map
row displays their locations. "Yes, we
borders," Okoye responds as she puts
en stares out the car's window at the
walking, stammering, or running.
several times to adjust her eyes to the
he atmosphere. A faint glow in the
s if they are all entering a smoky red
over at the captain, who seems to be

making their way out of the party when Okoye catches up to Lucinda. "Thank you," she says, gently touching the woman's arm.

Lucinda turns to face her and says, "You can thank me by convincing your king to come to the ribbon-cutting celebration for our new community center in Brownsville tomorrow. I've already invited everyone in this room, except him. He has a fortress of greedy investors and shameless politicians around him."

"I can do that. But first, what business do you have here?" Okoye asks.

"I'm the councilwoman out of one of the forgotten districts in Brooklyn—Brownsville—no-white-man's land, the edge of the world where poor and working-class people have been pushed to make way for people like the ones in this room in the affluent districts in Brooklyn. You know, I think you'll find lots of similarities to Wakanda in Brownsville. Just . . . come take a look around. The kids would love to see someone from Africa. And maybe you can learn a thing or two about Brownsville—the real Brooklyn and not the version they show on TV and in movies. They don't know much about Wakanda, but maybe you can school them."

Okoye extends her hand toward her and says, "I am Okoye."

"Thank you . . . sis," Lucinda says, taking her hand and giving it a firm shake.

"Captain, I think we should accept Lucinda Tate's invitation. She reached out to me personally and called me little sis and pointed out that there were only three of us there. That cocktail party was nothing like Saturday morning market in Wakanda, where all we see is deep brown skin," Okoye says to Aneka the following day as they dress for the next lineup of meetings and conferences.

"We have a gala to attend this evening at the Brooklyn Museum," Aneka says. "I don't know if the king is able to schedule a visit to . . ."

"Brownsville. That woman says it's like Wakanda. Maybe we could use a little bit of something like home while we're here."

Aneka steps closer to face Okoye directly. "Orders," she says. "*We* are the ones to follow orders from the king. And I am the one who gives you orders, not the other way around. Besides, these Americans have a very different idea of Wakanda in their minds. I'm guessing that it will be nothing like home."

Okoye inhales, stares directly at Aneka, and says, "It

is a *netwo*
haps it i:
whatevei

"You
you have
says, stari

The long,
is even m
slit along
but the wh
fight while
is not a sp
der the ki
a favorite t
know the t
who leads

"Ah! Br
out of the ti
off the Bro
Pedestrians
towering bu
and music o
"Reminds m

"Except too ma
pressed by it all.
"You are correc
energy, yes?"
In just minutes
of sleek condomini
changes. Within a
ings, row homes, a
ransacked and bor
line the fronts of s
bags are pushed t
so many sirens—e
Pitkin Avenue.
"There are few
Aneka asks, glanci
"Are we still i
Okoye discreet
bracelet and holds
appears and an ar
are still within its
away the bead, th
people standing,
Okoye blinks
slight change in
air makes it feel
bubble. She looks

just as bewildered by the strange sight. "Do you see that?" Okoye whispers to Aneka.

Aneka only furrows her brow and nods.

The SUV pulls up to a wide, newly renovated building that stands out in the middle of an empty, gated lot. A long red ribbon is tied across a set of double glass doors and beside it is Lucinda Tate dressed in a pair of jeans, sneakers, and a green T-shirt that reads *A Tree Grows in Brownsville*.

Lucinda hesitantly bows and sings, "Your Highness!"

"Please," King T'Chaka says as he steps out of the truck. "No need for that, Ms., uh . . . I'm afraid I didn't get your name."

Lucinda walks over to the king and extends a hand. "Lucinda Tate and—"

"No one ever calls her Lucy," Okoye says, finishing her sentence.

"Good to see you again, Okoye. And you must be . . ."

"Aneka."

"Aneka. Pleasure to meet you."

"Where are the others?" the captain asks, looking around the barren block. Few cars drive by. An old man sits on an overturned crate in front of a nearby corner store with broken blinking lights.

Lucinda starts to wring her hands, inhales, licks

her lips, and says, "They must be running late. I've got RSVPs from . . ." She sighs. "Why don't we start? The kids will be here any minute."

"Please tell me more about this community center," King T'Chaka says.

"Well, this building is the newest structure we've been able to build here in Brownsville. You see, with lots of people moving out and homes being destroyed, all that tax money is going elsewhere. Schools are closing, businesses are leaving. I wanted this place to be a beacon of hope for what the future can be for these kids. We'll offer classes and workshops—"

Before Lucinda can finish, a horn suddenly blows in the distance, followed by a drum. Soon a marching band playing a familiar tune appears: Kids in blue-and-white uniforms holding large instruments turn the corner and make their way over to the building. A line of six girls wearing sky-blue leotards and white boots dance and twirl batons.

Okoye can't help but bob her head to the music, but as soon as the kids reach the front of the building, the music slows, then comes to a full stop. The marching band members lower their instruments and stare at Okoye, Aneka, and King T'Chaka.

"Are we too early?" a girl holding a horn by her side asks Lucinda. "You said everybody would be here."

"No, no, no! Don't stop the music. It's a celebration!" Lucinda says, rushing over to the band and motioning for them to keep playing.

But another girl in front of the dance line holds up her hand toward the band. "No! We are not performing for an audience of . . ." She looks Okoye, Aneka, and King T'Chaka up and down. "Three of your friends."

"Lucinda, I thought you said everybody and their mama was gonna be here. You said kings and presidents were coming to this ribbon-cutting celebration. But you got two of your cousins and your uncle to dress up all fancy for this just so we don't feel bad? That's wrong, Lucinda," the horn player says.

"No, no, wait!" Lucinda says. "These are not my friends or cousins or whatever. I want you to meet the ruler of the great Wakanda, King T'Chaka, and his . . . um . . ."

"Fashion models," Aneka says.

"Bodyguards," Okoye corrects her.

"Fashion model bodyguards?" the girl asks. "You mean to tell me this grown man has these two teenage girls protecting him?"

Okoye and Aneka exchange looks. Then Aneka says, "We are students training to be bodyguards, yes. And . . . we make some money on the side as fashion models."

Okoye furrows her brow at Aneka, but she knows better than to question her captain in front of strangers. The king doesn't seem to mind her little fib, anyhow.

"What part of Brooklyn is Wakanda, anyway?" a boy asks, walking up to Okoye with his drum extending out in front of him.

"Ah, Wakanda is a beautiful African nation with some of the kindest people in the world," King T'Chaka says, stepping closer to the boy. "You would be a great drummer there. In Wakanda, those who beat the drum are powerful because they control sound, which controls the crowd."

"Yeah, whatever. You trying to push us out of our neighborhood just like everybody else?" the boy asks. "I'm not trying to go to Wakanda, I'm staying right here in Brownsville."

"And what's Wakanda gonna do for Brownsville, anyway?" one of the dancers asks.

Both Okoye and Aneka quickly step in front of the king as if this girl is a threat.

"All right, everyone," Lucinda interrupts. "Look, I'm not gonna sugarcoat anything for you. But this is who showed up, and I want you all to show them some respect."

"No need to chastise them, Lucinda," the king says,

gently motioning for the Dora Milaje to step aside. "Please, show us the community center we are celebrating. I will give you my blessings so we can be on our way."

"Blessings? I hope they're the kind that comes with a comma and a bunch of zeros," the horn player says. The others start to remove their instruments to place them on the ground.

"King T'Chaka, we are pleased to open our fully renovated community center," Lucinda says as she pulls scissors from a nearby box. "We've worked so hard to get this. With all the schools shutting down and the kids being bused to other neighborhoods, this community center can bring some hope back to Brownsville. And maybe, with some more funding from the city and a generous donor, we can add a library and bring in some counselors. We'll get some supplies for murals and have concerts and family game nights. Brownsville will come alive again."

But Okoye and Aneka again step in between her and King T'Chaka before she can even hand him the scissors. Aneka grabs the scissors from Lucinda. "What is your plan for this?" she asks.

"I guess you two really are bodyguards, huh?" Lucinda says. "King T'Chaka, we would love for you to do the honors of cutting the ribbon."

"No, we would not *love* for you to do the honors," the girl with the horn says. "Lucinda, where are the money people? That building needs desks and chairs and computers. . . . This king doesn't look like he makes that kinda bank."

Okoye starts to say something to defend her king's honor, but there is nothing to say. There is no place for truth here—that Wakanda has its own banks, its own money, its own resources so that whatever these kids want, Wakanda is capable of providing ten times over.

A rumbling starts in the distance, and Okoye looks behind her to see a small crowd forming on the sidewalk and on the street. Local residents have gathered around for the celebration, but from the looks on their faces, it's clear that this is not the celebration they were hoping for.

"Where are all those politicians you promised, Lucinda?" someone calls out from the crowd.

King T'Chaka turns to the crowd and says, "I am the king of Wakanda. Thank you, Brownsville, for your warm hospitality."

"Wakanda? Wakanda ain't got no money!" another person shouts.

The crowd noise grows into a chorus of boos and insults. The kids in the marching band start to walk away to join the crowd.

"King T'Chaka, let's continue. I know you have somewhere to go," Lucinda pleads. "Do us the honor of cutting this ribbon."

The king hesitantly takes the giant scissors, but before he can cut the ribbon, someone yells from the crowd, "Get outta here, you bunch of dusty Africans! Y'all can't help us!"

"Ah!" Okoye calls out, leaping toward the crowd with a locked elbow and clenched fist, her eyes darting about in search of the perpetrator.

"Hey!" Lucinda steps in front of Okoye. "Relax. I don't want you to get hurt."

Okoye chuckles. "Get hurt by whom?" she says.

But Lucinda has already moved away, and the crowd starts to boo even louder. Okoye relaxes her stance while Aneka takes the scissors from the king and hands them to Lucinda. Aneka motions for the king to make his way back to the truck, where the driver has been sitting behind locked doors.

Okoye spots the two girls from the marching band— one with her arms crossed staring straight at Okoye, the other with a stream of tears running down her cheeks. Okoye's heart sinks. She swallows hard to get ahold of herself and follows the king and Aneka back into the truck.

"Hey, King T'Chaka," Lucinda calls out. "I'm really

sorry about this. You gotta understand. We're desperate for some help here, and you were the only ones to show up. We were expecting an army of—"

But the door to the SUV slams shut before Okoye, Aneka, and the king can hear what Lucinda has to say. Someone throws something at their window, and then another. The chorus of boos follows them out of Brownsville.

"What a waste of time," Aneka says. "Never have you been so disrespected, my king."

Okoye turns back to get one last look at that dilapidated Brownsville street and the crowd in the distance. The new community center is a stark contrast to everything around it with its sparkling windows and futuristic design. A nearby park adds a stretch of green foliage to the surrounding brown and gray colors of the buildings. One of the girls still has her eyes on their truck, and it's almost as if she can still see Okoye, too— as if she wants to come with them, or she doesn't want them to leave.

"My king, are you all right?" Okoye asks.

King T'Chaka nods. "I will be okay," he says. "What is this place again?"

"Brownsville," Okoye says softly. "Brownsville, Brooklyn."

She has to adjust her eyes once more as the red glow

in the air begins to dissipate. It's as if they've just exited a fog. As they drive through other parts of Brooklyn, it becomes clear to Okoye that Brownsville does feel similar to Wakanda. Some sort of force is keeping it isolated, or maybe in danger. No matter. This is none of Okoye's business. At the very least, she's gotten to see a well-hidden part of this city, so she is now a much wiser and well-traveled Dora Milaje. Like Captain Aneka. Almost.

CHAPTER 5

"You should never have brought us there," Captain Aneka says when they arrive at the Brooklyn Museum. The huge structure spreads across an entire block, and its facade is a mix of old-world Europe with its Roman architecture and New World Brooklyn with its glass entryway and outdoor band performances. Inside, a number of guests have come to greet the king with smiles and handshakes. Okoye and Aneka are trailing a few feet behind, keeping watch on everything as usual.

"How could I have known, Captain? At least that woman was very kind," Okoye responds.

"No one here is that kind, Okoye. She wanted something from us."

"Ha! So you agree with me. You don't trust Lucinda Tate in the same way that I do not trust Stella Adams."

"Stella Adams has not put the king in danger," Aneka whispers.

"Yet. She has not put the king in danger *yet*."

"Stand down, Okoye. This entire trip is on Stella Adams's dime on behalf of NNLB. No one here intends to harm the king," Aneka says through clenched teeth.

"No matter where we are in the world, we will always be Dora Milaje," Okoye says, lowering her voice to a whisper. "But that place . . . I apologize for leading the king there."

"Well, he was not harmed," Aneka says. "But Brownsville isn't so different from the shantytowns in Soweto or Lagos."

"But in Wakanda the children show respect," Okoye says. "That is how I was raised in the village— to respect elders and our peers and, most importantly, royalty."

"How many times must I tell you, Okoye? This is not Wakanda. America could never be Wakanda."

"Clearly," Okoye mumbles. "But what do you make of that red atmosphere, eh, Captain? It is as if there is something keeping that place separate from the rest of the city."

"Who knows, Okoye," the captain says. "Air pollution. Too much noise. Too many people. It isn't our concern."

Captain Aneka walks away to engage in a bit of a light conversation with the attendees. Okoye is about to join her, but she spots the tall blond woman out of the corner of her eye. Stella Adams is wearing a long, fitted black gown and her bleached-blond hair is pulled back into a sleek bun. Her lips are bloodred and her eyes are glued to the king. Again.

Okoye quickens her pace to reach the king before Stella does, but Aneka places her arm in front of her. Okoye looks down at the captain's arm and then at her. "What is this for?"

"I am accompanying our king to this lovely gala," says Aneka. "I am going to mingle and smile and laugh at stupid jokes. And you are going to take a taxi back to the hotel to get your mind off things for a bit. You will join us in the morning. Please, Okoye. Do this for yourself and do this for us. I know how you feel. I was once new to this place and had to adjust very quickly. Take this evening off. Go to the gym. Sit in the Jacuzzi. Watch American television. Anything."

"So this is a vacation after all?" asks Okoye.

"This is a humanitarian trip," Aneka says. "Be humane to yourself first."

Okoye exhales and pivots toward the front entrance, hikes up her dress, and as soon as she steps outside the museum, she kicks off her heels and holds them in her hand as she walks out to the curb. The concrete is cool and smooth beneath her bare feet, unlike the prickly grass, moist soil, and rocky roads of her childhood in Wakanda.

The late spring air is warm against her deep brown skin, and the evening sky holds the promise of a full moon and barely visible twinkling stars. The streets are crowded with bodies moving about, and shiny cars form a line in front of the museum picking up and dropping off people in tuxedos and gowns. Okoye pauses, relaxes her shoulders, and inhales Brooklyn's air, thick with stories and unspoken truths. As a Dora Milaje, she's learned to read everything about the space and people surrounding her. So she looks past the fancy people attending a gala to raise money for the poor people and broken places around the world, and sees the poor people and broken places right here in New York City, right here in Brooklyn, and right on this wide, busy street called Eastern Parkway.

She spots a nearby couple on a stroll and asks, "Excuse me, how far is it to get to Brownsville?"

"Brownsville?" the woman asks. "Never heard of it." She's petite with a dark pixie cut and large green eyes.

For a second, Okoye wonders if this Brownsville is invisible to some people in the same way that the true Wakanda is unknown to the neighboring African nations. She walks down a few blocks until she spots a group of teenagers hanging out in front of a corner store on Franklin Avenue. The neighborhood is different here—not quite like Brownsville and worlds apart from the gala at the museum. She stops in front of them, staring.

"Wrong party, queen," a girl from the group says. "You look like a broke Black Cinderella who made a wrong turn."

"Brokerella!" a boy calls out, and they all laugh.

Heat rises from the pit of Okoye's belly and reaches her head, making her feel like she's about to explode. Every muscle in her body is telling her to defend her honor, and she certainly would be within her rights to do so. These kids are her age. They are her peers and they are just standing there, laughing at her. This is not a real threat, as Captain Aneka would assure her. But still, she feels the heat of rage pooling on top of her head, so she yanks off her wig to cool down.

"Oh snap! More like Balderella!" the boy says, and they laugh even louder and harder. "And what's with all those tattoos?"

"Have you no manners?" Okoye shouts above their laughter.

They quiet down. "Manners? What planet are you from?" a girl asks.

"Not a planet, but a nation. Wakanda," Okoye responds.

They laugh even more. "You're a long way from Wakanda, sis."

"Then how far is it to get to Brownsville?" Okoye asks.

"Brownsville? You're trying to go to Brownsville looking like that?" the boy says. "You might as well go back to Wakanda, Balderella."

Okoye steps closer. "I was already in Brownsville, and the kids there, they are just like you."

"Of course they're just like us. They're Black, we're Black, you're Black. But it's different out there. I got cousins from Brownsville and ever since they started using that drug, things never been the same," the boy says.

Okoye steps closer. "Drug?"

"Fall back, Balderella," the girl says. "You're getting too close, and you look mad thirsty. That's probably why you're going there in the first place—to get some of that Bliss."

Another girl shushes her, and they start looking about as if expecting something or someone. "Are you kidding me right now?" the girl says. "She could be . . ."

The kids freeze for a moment, staring at Okoye for a long second. Then, slowly, they start to walk away from the corner store and disperse, leaving Okoye standing there in a ball gown, clutching her high heels in one hand and her wig in the other.

"How far is it to get to Brownsville?" Okoye calls out one more time.

None of the kids answer. Okoye starts to walk away, but an old man wearing tattered clothes and worn sneakers sitting on an overturned plastic crate says with a raspy voice, "Don't mention that PyroBliss over here."

"PyroBliss?" Okoye asks.

"What'd I say? You're trying not to go back to Wakanda or wherever you came from?"

Okoye blinks several times, attempting to say the right thing. Here, no one is direct. No one says what they mean and means what they say. Dusk is slowly turning into night and the streets are getting louder. "Brownsville," she whispers, just in case that word is forbidden, too.

"The Three train to the last stop," the old man says, and drops his head as if he's suddenly fallen asleep.

"PyroBliss," Okoye whispers to herself as she walks to the train station with her heels making that annoying click-clack sound. She looks around, wondering if this PyroBliss is a special kind of power-enhancing plant like the heart-shaped herb. A drug, they call it.

CHAPTER 6

Brownsville is like a magnet, and Okoye feels the strong pull back to that place even when everything in her soul is telling her to be still, rest, and prepare for the next day of being by King T'Chaka's and Captain Aneka's sides. No matter. Aneka told her to take a break for the evening and this is how she wants to spend one night of this vacation—finding out why those kids reacted that way at the ribbon-cutting celebration. There is a stirring in her belly that tells her something wasn't right, and she wants to find out exactly what it is. Her Dora Milaje instincts are tugging at her nerves, and she has to pursue this nagging feeling about Brownsville.

The people were expecting something more, something greater. Okoye wants to let them know that

Wakanda has everything they could ever want. Of course, she must be discreet in revealing what Wakanda truly is to this very small part of the world, but there has to be another way to give some hope back to those people, those children. Maybe it will be enough that she returns to let them know that someone cares—that she cares.

Still wearing her dress from the gala and with her heels back on, clicking as she walks, Okoye doesn't take a seat on the subway train; she stands, not even holding on to a pole. She's made it this far even without having what they call a MetroCard and having to jump over a turnstile in a dress and heels. She had to ask several people for directions to the 3 train. The most challenging part of this ride is the men who stare and wink and smile too wide at her. The people on the train are of all races, shapes, and sizes, and it seems as if the entire world is represented in this single subway car. Most of them seem kind or simply tired and aloof. Others are rude and gesture at her in a way that would be taboo in Wakanda. If only she could wield her spear just once so they would take their eyes off her. But what's worse is what she hears and sees from the young people her age—teenagers who seem to run this whole city with their joy, laughter, playfulness, taunts, and insults.

"What are you looking at?" a girl wearing a short

dress with sneakers standing with a group of teenagers calls out to her.

"You. I am looking at you," Okoye says firmly with her eyes steady on the girl.

"Careful. You're asking for it," a woman in a nearby seat says, cautioning Okoye.

The group steps closer to Okoye in unison, staring hard without saying a word.

"What are you going to do, eh? Keep staring. You do not threaten me," Okoye says.

"Oh dear, here we go," the woman says, and scoots farther away from the oncoming drama.

"Is she for real?" the girl asks the other kids. "I know this bald-headed girl didn't just—"

"Wait a minute," another girl wearing a denim jacket and baseball cap says. "I've seen you before."

Okoye steps back a little, knowing that without her wig, she should be unrecognizable to anyone who had seen her at events with the king, but then she also recognizes the girl. She was the one with the horn—the one who was the most disappointed in seeing Okoye there.

"You came to Brownsville this afternoon to cut the ribbon."

"Well, no, I was not going to cut the ribbon. But yes, I was there."

"You know Lucinda Tate?"

Okoye pauses for a long second. Then she says, "Yes."

"Leave her alone, then," the girl says, motioning her friends to step away.

The group reluctantly steps back without taking their eyes off Okoye.

The train begins to slow down, and the conductor announces that it's Sutter Avenue and Rutland Road. The doors slide open to an overhead view of Brownsville. The train tracks are high above the buildings and trees here, and the sign reads NEW LOTS AVENUE. The group rushes out, laughing and shouting at one another even louder, their voices echoing across the nearly empty aboveground subway platform.

But the girl with the jacket stays back. "If you're looking for Lucinda, her office is a few blocks from the subway station on Pitkin Avenue," she says. "And if you're looking for a job at the new community center, she won't have any money to pay you and it'll probably be burned down by next week. But if you're looking for something else, I'll be around." The girl starts to run to catch up with her friends.

"Wait! What do you mean *burned down*?" Okoye asks.

The girl stops, turns around, and walks back toward Okoye. "Fine. Follow me. And don't be too nosy. Just mind your own business, all right?"

Okoye nods, relieved to have someone accompany

her, and it's definitely not because she's scared, and she definitely won't be minding her own business. This girl walks the streets with her head held high, her hands in her jacket's pockets, and taking quick, wide steps as if she owns this place. Her braided hair is pulled up on top of her head, and her eyes look as if they've seen too much and know too much for her age. Okoye only watches her, making sure that she doesn't say anything too soon that would make the girl abandon her. Maybe she will have an ally here.

The sun is nearly setting, so that strange red glow is even more visible. This redness was certainly not anywhere around the museum or near the hotel in Midtown. So Brownsville definitely has a look to it. Okoye sniffs and holds out her hand in the air, wondering if this redness is something she can also smell and feel. It looks as if this girl doesn't notice it, or maybe she is used to it. But Okoye will give her some time before she asks any questions.

It's also warmer here, as if the red color is what is left behind after a blazing fire. Streetlights line the sidewalks but only a few bulbs are working. More people are hanging out in front of buildings than earlier, as if sundown is the busiest time here. The ground is filthier, too. Broken glass, plastic bags, and garbage are everywhere. Okoye has no choice but to keep her heels on. The girl is walking quickly, ignoring Okoye and ready to return to whatever activities she had planned for the night. Okoye searches for this building where Lucinda Tate has her office. But most of the storefronts are padlocked with graffiti strewn across the gray metal gates and brick walls.

In the distance, on the next block, light shines out of a large window, and Okoye makes out the last two letters of the storefront's sign: TE. The girl is a few steps ahead of her, so she's rushing to her side when a sudden loud boom stops her in her tracks, followed by a chorus of cheers as if someone has set off fireworks. Soon smoke is visible in the dusk sky, then a spark of blue-orange colors light the air.

"What was that?" Okoye says.

"Mind your business, Baldilocks!" the girl sings.

"You can at least tell me your name," Okoye says. "After all, I am a long way from home walking with a stranger."

"I'm the one with a stranger. You're in *my* hood, remember?"

"I am Okoye."

"Okay?"

"O-ko-ye," she repeats, as she tries to keep up with the girl.

"I'm just gonna call you Okay, okay?" She stops at a

corner where a group of boys are hanging out. One of them starts to approach her, but she quickly shoos him away.

"No. That is not okay. Learn my name. Five letters, three syllables. O-KO-YE."

"Who do you think you are, girl? You're not from around here."

They cross the street. Okoye remains vigilant, observing everything around her. The people sitting on stoops, hanging from windows, and slowly walking by eye Okoye suspiciously. "And what is *your* name?" Okoye asks.

"Tree. Tree Foster," she says. "Now whoever sent you to poke around here, tell 'em my name, if they don't already know."

"That is your name? Tree?" Okoye asks.

"Tree. Four letters, one syllable."

"Like a tree grows in Brownsville," Okoye says, remembering what was on Lucinda's T-shirt earlier. Okoye notices the fire in Tree's eyes. She is fierce. In another place, Tree could be training to become a Dora Milaje. She is a warrior indeed. "Why do they call you that? A tree?"

"Seriously? I have to spell out everything for these foreigners? Because I'm like a tree, that's why. We're all like trees. We've been here forever and we're deeply rooted. Our branches spread far and wide. We're planted here and even if we're ever uprooted, our seeds will still be here and more *trees* will be planted."

Okoye nods and smiles, feeling a sudden kinship with Tree. "So I can be a tree, too? Deeply rooted with my branches spreading far and wide?"

Tree laughs. "I mean, you're here, right? Traveling to a whole other country and all. Not a lot of kids like me from around here get to do that."

They reach the office and a door swings open and Lucinda Tate ushers them in.

"Slow your roll, young bodyguard. You've come back to save us?" Lucinda says.

"We don't need anyone claiming to be our saviors, Lucinda," Tree says.

"Yes. Well, I am here on the orders of King T'Chaka. He'd like to know more about Brownsville," Okoye lies.

"Huh. Most girls your age are on dates or getting ready for a party, but here you are, supermodel bodyguard following orders from your king."

"Lucinda, *I'm* not going on a date or getting ready for a party," Tree says, cocking her head and crossing her arms over her chest.

Okoye clears her throat and asks, pointing her chin toward what looks like an explosion outside the office windows, "What is happening there?"

"Oh, just another night in Brownsville," Lucinda says just as sirens go off in the distance.

"I gotta go," Tree says, looking back nervously. "The rest of the crew is waiting for me."

"No!" Lucinda says. "I . . . I need some help around here before I close."

Tree stares at Lucinda wide-eyed and with clenched teeth. "Are you kidding me, Lucinda?" She quickly glances at Okoye.

"Sorry. I mean . . . fine. Go ahead. Just . . . be safe out there."

Okoye's brow furrows, but she quickly relaxes her face, making sure to keep her concerns hidden. After all, a Dora Milaje must remain cool, calm, and unaffected by their surroundings. Okoye is still learning, but she's glad the lessons have stuck so that she's able to constantly correct herself.

Tree exhales and crosses her arms. "All right, Lucinda. I'll help out. What do you need me to do?"

"Look around," Lucinda says. "I know it's not a lot, but twenty for the hour?"

Tree surveys the office, trying to avoid eye contact with Okoye. "I don't need the money, Lucinda," she says.

Lucinda flashes the girl a reprimanding glare, but she quickly spreads a smile across her face when her eyes meet Okoye's. The councilwoman's office is shabby and messy, with desks covered with file folders and coffee cups, trash cans overflowing, and newspaper clippings lining the walls. So Tree starts to clean up. Okoye instinctively tries to help.

"What are you doing?" Lucinda says. "I know you didn't come all the way out here to clean my office, unless you could use twenty dollars."

Okoye starts to say something, but a blaring sound cuts through the other noises on the Brownsville streets.

"I'm surprised they got here so fast," Lucinda mumbles. "The mayor thinks the city should let us burn."

"Why are those trucks so loud?" Okoye asks, wondering if those are armed vehicles and slightly embarrassed that she has to ask so many questions. A quick peek at her Kimoyo bead would've given her any answers she needed right now.

"Oh my goodness!" Tree exclaims. "Y'all don't have fire trucks in Africa?"

"Of course they do," Lucinda says to the girl. Then she turns to Okoye. "You're a little too dressed up for a visit to Brownsville."

"I just came from a gala. I wanted to come here before tonight. Tomorrow will be busy. Tell me, Lucinda Tate. What is going on here?"

"You really want me to answer that question?"

"If she really wants to know, she can start by reading these," Tree says as she gathers newspapers into a pile.

Okoye stares at the newspapers. Although she's not opposed to reading, a Kimoyo bead would be able to synthesize all that information. No matter. She would rather hear the truth from the people who live here. "Lucinda, the people of Brownsville look like the people back home in Wakanda. Those kids can be my brothers and sisters, and it is clear that there is something happening here that is hurting their hearts and minds. Maybe there is something my king can do. Sometimes I think we can do more . . . but it is not in my control. But I am here now," Okoye says firmly. "What do you need?"

"First of all, let's get one thing clear, young lady. This is not Africa. Don't come out here thinking you could wave some magic Wakandan wand and all our problems will go away."

"Try me."

The girl laughs and walks closer to Okoye. "Are you serious? Look out that window. You see that smoke over there? You get closer, you'll see an entire building up in flames."

"We should go help!" Okoye says.

"And what are *you* going to do? Huh?" Tree continues, holding up one of the newspapers. "You see this red air all around here? Once Stella Adams and NNLB started to buy up all these properties in Brownsville, they left behind a little something for us to remember them by. When the buildings go up in flames from the PyroBliss serum, they leave behind a red tint in the sky. And it stays up there like some sort of red bubble around all of Brownsville. Even when there aren't any fires and things are quiet for a while, everything stays red. It's like a stain we can't remove."

"PyroBliss serum? So is it medicine or poison?" Okoye asks.

"Depends on who you ask," Tree says. She points to a photo of Stella Adams in one of the articles.

Okoye quickly reads the headline: "NNLB Is Saving the City One Neighborhood at a Time."

"This is a good thing, no?" Okoye asks, pointing to the paper in Tree's hand.

"No! It's making us all sick," Tree continues. Her mood has shifted. Beads of sweat form on her forehead, and she steps closer to Okoye. "We tried to let the media know, but that red air doesn't show up on cameras. You have to be here to see it and believe it. And those buildings going up in flames . . . it's not just fire. It's something more—something worse, as if Brownsville is slowly starting to look like hell."

Lucinda touches the girl gently on her shoulder as if

to calm her down. "Yeah, she's right. Okoye, whatever's going on in Wakanda, you just stepped out of the frying pan and into the fire. Can't take the heat, get out the kitchen. People who want to stop all this burning call the fire trucks, but they don't come fast enough. We've complained to our politicians, written petitions, but it's like no one is hearing us outside this red bubble. Some may call me Brownsville's super hero, but I can't put out fires—literally or figuratively. And especially not after that tired ribbon-cutting celebration. My people wore me out today."

"Don't put it all on your people, Lucinda," Tree says. "Stella Adams and NNLB should've come through. Once they found out that you didn't want any of their money for the community center, she didn't even want to show her face around here. So much for saving Brownsville."

"And so much for telling me to mind my own business," Okoye says. "There is a lot happening here and you say that NNLB is not helping. How is that possible when they are supposed to be saving the city? After all, this is why they invited my king here in the first place."

Tree starts to say something, but Lucinda holds up her hand. "Tree, whatever you're about to say, y'all sound just as ignorant when y'all talk about Africa."

"Why are we telling her all this, anyway? What can *she* do?" Tree asks.

Lucinda exhales and plops down on a nearby desk chair. "Look, Okoye. I get it. You're from a whole other culture, so let me school you. It's called PyroBliss. The kids take it. And when there's enough of it in their system, there's nothing that can stop them from setting the world on fire. Literally. The bliss is in seeing things burn. The colors, the heat . . . it all does something to them. I don't know what it is. Never tried it and never will. Plus, it's not going to work on me. I'm too old. But it's ravaged this community like a plague. The city knows about it, but it's like they want us trapped in here until it all burns down. Then they'll build on top of all our ashes."

Tree is staring at Lucinda with rage written all over her face. "It's none of her business," she says through clenched teeth.

"You brought her over here, Tree. Don't you want the world to know what's happening here? Well, she's from the world."

"Wakanda, or wherever she's from, is not the world."

"PyroBliss," Okoye interrupts. "You can just put out the fires, no?"

Tree exhales and rolls her eyes. "It's not even real

fire. At least, not the kind we're used to. Fire burns when you touch it. It spreads. But with PyroBliss, it only affects structures, as if its only purpose is to burn down homes. I mean, it's a good thing that it doesn't harm people. But in a roundabout way, it does because we're hurt when our homes are destroyed."

Okoye smiles a little, knowing that this girl is sharing when she doesn't have to. "Thank you, Tree Foster. I know you don't think Wakanda can do much, but—"

"But nothing," Tree says. "Now that you know, you better leave us alone. This ain't no tourist stop."

"I understand, but you are telling me not to trust Stella Adams and NNLB."

"Okoye," Lucinda interjects. "We don't want to put you in any compromising position. Tree is right. Just be careful and know that it's not all about world peace and ending poverty with those people. You should know that, being from Africa and all."

Okoye's mind is swirling with questions. Her first instinct is to pull out a Kimoyo bead since all this was not part of Captain Aneka's briefing. But she'd be revealing too much in front of these strangers. It's getting harder and harder for Okoye to hide almost every aspect of her true self, even when it would be useful. But she is soon distracted by something she sees outside the office. A group of kids are huddled together on a corner across the street. She slowly opens the door, but before she can step foot onto the sidewalk, a fight breaks out. Tree rushes past her to get to the group, and Okoye is at her heels just as Lucinda yells, "Stay out of it, Okoye!"

Some of the kids disperse seconds before Tree and Okoye reach them. Always quick to notice the smallest movements, Okoye spots a bag of tiny bottles changing hands. The few kids that are left form a semicircle as if protecting something or someone behind them.

"We're good here, super hero," Tree says. "These are my friends."

"She's the same lady that came here to cut that ribbon but turned her back on us," a girl says, eyeing Okoye up and down. "Tree, who is she? You looking for something, Baldy?"

"She's nobody," Tree says. "What's going on with Mars?"

"Why were you fighting?" Okoye asks, observing everything about them. Their clothes, hair, and shoes look as if these kids are ready for combat, as if there is a war brewing and they were born prepared to fight it.

Lucinda reaches Okoye just in time to pull her back, away from the kids. "Go on about your business, y'all. My friend here was just trying to help," she says.

Okoye looks down at Lucinda's hand wrapped

around her thin, muscular arm and then up at Lucinda, who quickly drops her hand.

"I told you to leave them alone," Lucinda whispers.

Okoye looks at Lucinda, slightly confused. But she holds her tongue as the kids start to leave. That's when she spots another girl—the one with the dress and sneakers from the train—hunched over, leaning on Tree. But still, Okoye doesn't say a word even though every part of her Dora Milaje soul wants to know what's wrong with that girl.

"Now that we've told you about what's happening here with PyroBliss, will you let your king know?" Lucinda asks. "Maybe he can nudge some of the other diplomats or get this info to some high-powered government official. They don't listen to us in this city, they don't hear us. At least you're seeing what's going on. Everything Tree said is true. I know they probably won't listen to you, either. But your king will. And they'll listen to him."

Okoye nods as if she's just received orders from her captain. "By the way, what was wrong with that girl?"

"Her name is Mars, and she's Tree's girlfriend," Lucinda says. "She took the PyroBliss serum, and she probably set that building on fire. That thing saps all your energy, and she's just about wiped out. They're hiding her."

"Why would she do that?" Okoye says. "If Tree is her girlfriend, doesn't she already know of the dangers?"

"You really are from another planet, huh? This is the hood, Okoye. Aren't there any ghettos in Wakanda? I know there are poor places all over Africa, but you're acting like you've never seen kids misbehaving and acting a fool. And unfortunately, they don't always make the right choices, like taking PyroBliss. It makes them do terrible things to themselves and their community. That's why I opened up a community center. They need treatment and counseling and attention and love. That's why we need help and we want the city and the entire world to take notice," Lucinda says in almost one breath.

"Huh," Okoye replies, frowning and looking all around the block. The sun has set and night creeps over the city like a shadow.

"Is that all you have to say?" Lucinda asks.

"I don't like to talk. I like to take action." Okoye starts to walk in the direction of the kids, but a black SUV parked on the corner stops her in her tracks. Someone is looking out of the back window, but she can't make out who. The window quickly rolls up and the SUV suddenly pulls away and speeds around the corner and up the block.

"Hmph. They're definitely not from around here," Lucinda says.

"Maybe they are police and they were here to help."

Lucinda starts to laugh, just like the kids. She keeps laughing, holds her belly, doubles over, and laughs some more.

"What is so funny?" Okoye asks.

"Wakanda must be in a whole other galaxy," Lucinda says, coughing and chuckling. But her laughter soon fades into a look of worry. She inhales deep and continues, "Seriously, sis. You are really out of touch. If you want to help, you have to know what's been going on around here and other places like this. I mean, there's things that you can't see so easily, you know?"

"No, I do not know," Okoye says firmly.

"Clearly. Come with me," Lucinda says, motioning for Okoye to follow her. "Look, PyroBliss came into this community from out of nowhere, it seems. It spread quickly, like wildfire. Literally. The kids push it, sell it, and take it, and they basically turn into pyromaniacs. It doesn't have the same effect on anyone over twenty-one. It's like the serum only preys on adolescent minds, just like how it only affects structures and homes. There's some kind of fiery energy in young people that the drug can tap into. It was designed that way. Get them young and impressionable. I guess whoever created it believed the kids would be more destructive, more prone to addiction. I hate everything about PyroBliss and the people behind it. The kids in this neighborhood are good kids. Really, they are. But . . ."

"This drug . . . it makes them do evil things, but they are not evil."

"Exactly! And I want you to be careful. I know you're from a whole other country and culture and all, but you're still their age. You and your friend are still susceptible to PyroBliss's effects," Lucinda says, stopping in front of a building that is completely burned-out. Windows are missing and the roof is gone. Black smoke stains the brick and the broken storefront sign.

"The kids did this?" Okoye asks.

"Well, yes and no. PyroBliss made them do this."

"Where can I find this PyroBliss?"

"Do not take it, Okoye! You're practically royalty. Most kids here don't get to travel with a king as a diplomat. Don't throw that all away, Okoye, just out of curiosity."

"I want to help. I want to get my king to help. The more information I have, the more I can share with King T'Chaka. Please. I'm sure there is something we can do."

Lucinda gives Okoye a once-over. "All right. But this information is for your king. You can find PyroBliss any and everywhere. In fact, the kids you just met would've handed it to you if you asked and paid the right price. But that's not the question you want to ask."

Okoye nods. "Ah, yes. You want to get rid of it. I want to get rid of it, too, if it is causing this much distress."

Lucinda inhales. Even in the dim streetlight, Okoye can see sadness passing over her face. Her locs hang over her shoulders in thick spirals and she's less made up than she was at the cocktail party—no mascara or lipstick—and looks much more tired than she did earlier today. "You make it sound so easy," she says. "Like we can actually get rid of it. Look. Your king has been all over the world, and he's seen crime and poverty. I'm sure you have crime and poverty in Wakanda. The news makes it seem as if your country has never been touched by colonization, that it's stuck in the past with all the goatherders and basket weavers and all."

Okoye turns slightly away so that Lucinda doesn't see the look of pure incredulity on her face. Indeed, the stories this country spins about Wakanda are just ridiculous. At the very least, they protect her beloved nation against greedy corporations and people who want to push things like PyroBliss onto the children. Okoye and the Dora Milaje would never allow that to happen, much less the king.

"But you know that it's not as simple as just kids making bad decisions," Lucinda continues. "Word on the street is that Stella and her company created and dropped PyroBliss into Brownsville. She uses the kids to push it onto their friends. In return, she gives them protection, money, and housing. But if this truth gets out, no one would believe me.

"Stella makes it seem as if she's this humanitarian saving the world with her husband's charity. But it's all one big lie. She wants the land and the real estate. She wants to build herself a *new* New York City right here in Brownsville. And she wants all of us out of her way. She's willing to do any and everything to wipe us out. Stella and her husband have this city in the palms of their hands, and they don't care what's happening here. Okoye, if your king can help in any way . . ."

"Stella Adams, eh? Well, yes, my king has traveled and has seen terrible things. To my understanding, just one person is never to blame. But you are blaming just one person for your problems here?"

"Well, of course it's a whole system. But Stella Adams seems to be pulling all the strings as far as Brownsville goes—she and her husband. You know how they say that the man is the head but the woman is the neck? Well, Stella is controlling everything. I've been watching her for years at galas and fundraising events, and at press conferences where she pretends to care. No Nation Left Behind Industries is funding the whole thing. And that SUV you just saw? She probably sent some of her goons over here."

"What were they here to do?"

Lucinda shakes her head. "To sniff around. To see who's playing the roles they've been assigned and who's trying to mess up their plans. I know you're too young to really understand all of this. But I'm telling you just like I've told Tree, Mars, and all the other kids around here. They have to know what's going on. And if they don't believe me, they eventually see it for themselves, just like Tree did. Then they start taking matters into their own hands. Some get it, others don't. Tree is trying to convince her friends that something ain't right, but she's only one kid. We need a critical mass to change things around here and in this city. I know you're not from Brownsville, and you're not even from this country, but it looks like you've got some sense. So which side are you on?" Lucinda asks.

"You are not being very clear," Okoye says.

Lucinda sighs. "I don't even know why I asked."

Okoye lets her have those last words. She has more questions, but Lucinda seems flustered and impatient with her. There is suffering and corruption here, but

Okoye wants to know why and how this came to be. Such things would never be allowed to take place in Wakanda. And if the king has witnessed this sort of instability in other parts of the world, then why hasn't he done anything about it, especially with all the resources Wakanda has? Okoye will find her own answers. If there is a problem, then she can find the solution. But all those skills as a Dora Milaje are reserved for King T'Chaka and Wakanda. Answers and solutions are not for some place called Brownsville, Brooklyn, in New York City. Why must she care so much, anyway?

Okoye has done everything to prepare for battle, any battle, as a Dora Milaje. But this battle, the one that is tugging at her core, making her question her allegiance, is one she was not expecting. No matter. Okoye, Captain Aneka, and the king will be leaving in a few days. There will be other problems, bigger problems, wherever they are headed next. If the king wants to help, fine. If not, she will be home soon and Brownsville will be a distant memory.

"Where's your fancy truck?" Lucinda asks on their way back to her storefront office.

"I took the subway," Okoye says.

"You're brave. Let me call you a cab."

"No. I can take the subway back. I want to get to

know this part of New York City, this part of the world."

"You just did. Same story in every hood around the world."

"Well." Okoye hesitates. Then she asks, "Do you live far? May I escort you home?"

Lucinda chuckles. "Child. You want to escort *me*? Thanks, but no thanks. I'm just a few blocks away. Brownsville born and raised, so I'm good."

"Is that right? Were you like those children? Did you not have a safe and happy childhood?"

Lucinda sighs, shaking her head. "You sound just like all the other well-meaning folks who come around here. They treat us like a science experiment—probing and prodding with all kinds of questions. Yes, I had a very happy childhood and safety is relative. Just because it looks like things have fallen apart here, doesn't mean that we are not happy. That's what you all do in Wakanda, too—make the best out of nothing and find joy in the slivers of light, the cracks in the pavement, the ashes on the ground. Feel me?"

Okoye swallows hard before saying, "Yes, I . . . We do the very best we can with what we have in Wakanda."

"I hope so," Lucinda says, pursing her lips. "Train's that way. Take it into the city. I'm sure you, the king, and your friend are staying in some fancy hotel. Enjoy your time here in the Big Apple, and tell His Highness

I said what's up, and . . . maybe I'll see you all again."

Okoye watches Lucinda walk away, and she crosses her arms as goose bumps form on her skin. If Okoye squints a little, Lucinda looks like one of the teenagers from behind. Glass breaks in the distance followed by enthusiastic cheering. Then an explosion. Okoye ducks but the fire is nowhere near her. She turns around to see bright orange-blue flames lighting the night sky again. Every cell in her body is telling her to run and search for the king. Every bit of danger that arises always has to do with the king. But King T'Chaka is miles away. Still, someone must be hurt. A child, maybe. She has to find out. She has to go and help. But the king . . .

It's late and she is still dressed for a fancy party. She checks her Kimoyo bead for the king's and the captain's whereabouts. They're both back at the hotel now. Aneka already knows where she is if she checked one of her own Kimoyo beads. It's a good thing that the king isn't pre-occupied with where they are, since it's their job to look out for him. But T'Chaka will be furious if he finds out how far she's gone. So Okoye forces herself back to the subway station and onto the number 3 train headed for Midtown Manhattan. Wakanda has won this tiny battle for her heart. But the war inside her has just begun—a mighty African nation versus a poor, struggling neigh-borhood in one of the most powerful countries in the world. As she stands in the middle of the train, more teenagers board, different ones this time. Again, they stare at her, make fun of her head and dress. She only stares back, unfazed. Part of her is impressed that some of these kids do not respect her, unlike the ones all over Africa. Still, Lucinda warned her not to judge. But it is not judgment, it is observation. It is what she's trained to do.

As the train approaches the city, it becomes louder and more crowded. The New Yorkers ignore her now, so she feels invisible. Okoye sighs. She's been trained to fight. She's prepared for small battles and big wars in defense of Wakanda. Wakanda is her world, and nothing else is supposed to exist outside it.

CHAPTER 7

"**S**o what were you doing in Brownsville?" Captain Aneka asks Okoye the next morning over breakfast.

The king is seated a few tables away, having a one-on-one meeting with the president of a small Caribbean nation. Okoye and Aneka are keeping their distance while closely watching the king, who is all smiles as he and his colleague sip coffee. Okoye doesn't touch her breakfast of scrambled eggs and diced vegetables. Heavy meals in the morning slow her down and blur her senses. Today, much like any other day, she has to be alert and focused for her king. But from the way Aneka is devouring her meal, Okoye feels as if she's the only one not on vacation.

"I went to see Lucinda," Okoye says plainly.

"Oh, that is not a pleasant night off. I suggested that you take a break, Okoye. What made you decide to go there?"

"I was . . . on a tour," Okoye says, finally taking a bite of her eggs and wanting to avoid Aneka's many questions.

Aneka only stares at her while eating, seemingly reading her thoughts.

"Tell me, Captain, where are these special humanitarian missions taking place?" Okoye asks.

"I know what you're thinking. Not in Brownsville, for sure."

"It's clear."

Aneka doesn't respond. Instead, she seems distracted by something she sees outside, through the large windows of the hotel's restaurant. Okoye knows not to turn around so as not to bring attention to whoever or whatever it is.

"Tell me," Okoye says.

"Our king has a fan," Aneka says.

Within seconds, Okoye is made aware of what Aneka has noticed. Out of the corner of her eyes she spots Stella Adams entering the restaurant. "Networking, eh?" Okoye says.

"Right. Networking," Aneka responds.

They both try to finish their breakfast, but Okoye and Aneka are distracted by Stella's loud laughter. It's as if she's putting on a show for the king. Years of training as Dora Milaje has taught them to be suspicious of such behavior—laughing too loud to conceal ulterior motives.

But Aneka shrugs and says, "She likes him."

"He is married," Okoye says.

"Americans don't care."

Okoye glances back at the king, who is joined only by Stella now. The Caribbean statesman has left. The woman is leaning in too close as if flirting with the king. Without hesitating, Okoye gets up from her seat and approaches her king.

"Is everything all right here?" she asks, towering over Stella.

Stella looks up and wipes the smile from her face. "We were just attending to some business matters," she says coolly. Then she extends her hand toward Okoye. "I don't believe we've met. Stella."

"We have met," Okoye says with an even colder voice and cutting off the king, who was about to introduce her. "Maybe in Brownsville."

Stella drops her hand. "Oh," she inhales. "You

must've met Lucinda Tate. Tell me, how was that, uh, ribbon-cutting party? I heard it's like a war zone out there. We had high hopes for Brownsville. But, those people . . . those kids . . . they can't seem to get it together over there. And Lucinda tries so hard. That poor girl must be exhausted."

Okoye cocks her head to the side. Stella's tone and her words have gotten under her skin. "Explain yourself."

"Okoye," says the king in a cautionary tone. Then he stands to meet her gaze and whispers, "Be cautious with your words. Charm and wit can disarm enemies."

Aneka is suddenly standing beside her, and she gently touches Okoye's arm as a way to cool her down. "My king. We apologize for the disruption. We just wanted to make sure that everything is all right."

King T'Chaka nods, Aneka touches Okoye's arm once again, and they begin to walk away.

Okoye overhears Stella saying to the king, "Bodyguards, huh? They're just schoolgirls. But I guess in some places like Wakanda that doesn't matter. Now, where can I get myself one or two of those?"

Okoye swallows hard, pushing back the urge to turn around and assert her power. She wishes she had her spear. Just holding it beside her and standing at attention next to her king would be enough to deter any evil intention—and Stella was brimming with mischief. But what kind of mischief? Okoye isn't sure. Maybe there's much more to Lucinda's story about Stella and PyroBliss. And if it is true, what business does Stella Adams have with the king, anyway?

Okoye doesn't say a word to Captain Aneka, who is eyeing her with suspicion.

"Surely you can't be suspicious of that blond woman?" Aneka finally asks when they're back at their table.

"I am," Okoye says.

"Sister, this is the American way. They smile to each other's faces as they do business over coffee or dinner. Remember our training session, Okoye? *Diplomacy*."

Okoye is quiet for a long moment while Aneka sips the rest of her tea. The faces of the kids in Brownsville are tattooed in her mind. She will never forget them. "Captain," she says. "Our king has not met with the *people*. He's been with heads of state and businessmen. But what about the people?"

"Huh. So that is what is weighing heavy on that big head of yours. First you chastise those people for attacking our king, now you want him to return there to meet with them?" Aneka says, patting the corners of her mouth with a napkin.

Before Okoye can respond, the two Dora Milaje

quickly stand at attention as Stella approaches their table.

"Relax, ladies. I'm a friend, not the enemy," Stella says. "I'd like to make a request. Let me have the king for a day. I'll take good care of him. You two lovely young ladies can have the day off. Visit NYU or Columbia University. Walk along Madison or Park or Fifth Avenue. Tiffany, Saks, and if you're being frugal, Macy's on Thirty-Fourth Street. And the boys will love you over in Times Square."

"We will accompany you and the king to wherever you are going," Okoye quickly says, ignoring Stella's suggestions.

Captain Aneka walks over to King T'Chaka, who is signing the check. Okoye doesn't move, locked in a staring match with Stella, who steps closer to her. Okoye can smell her breath, she is that close.

"Be careful wandering those streets of Brownsville all alone," Stella whispers. "I hear Wakanda's a lovely place, and I'm sure you'd want to return. In one piece."

Okoye clenches her fist, and her whole body tenses up.

"Okoye!" Aneka says from beside King T'Chaka.

Okoye swallows hard and exhales as Stella steps back and smiles.

"It's been decided," Aneka says. "We will accompany the king."

"Oh, that's too bad," Stella says, turning back to face King T'Chaka. "We'll have to reschedule, then, or I might have to steal you away."

"Eh?" Okoye says, stepping closer to Stella once again.

"Wow. I'm impressed, King T'Chaka. You've trained them well."

King T'Chaka furrows his brow, clearly upset at what Stella has just said. "With all due respect, Ms. Adams, I did not train these brilliant young women. They are wise and powerful in their own right, even if they were once village girls. We hold our women and girls in high esteem in Wakanda. Please let me know if you'd like me to share our best practices with NNLB. They are my responsibility just as I am theirs. Do I make myself clear, Ms. Adams?"

A polite smile spreads across Stella's face. "I didn't mean any disrespect, Your Highness," she says. She nods at Okoye and Aneka, then struts out of the restaurant, leaving the king and the Dora to attend to the rest of their diplomatic responsibilities.

"Are you sure you want to be in business with her, my king?" Okoye asks.

Aneka shoots her a look, as if to say that it is none of *her* business.

"Diplomacy, Dora Milaje," King T'Chaka says as they walk out of the hotel's restaurant. "Diplomacy is the name of the game. Show kindness and respect, even when it isn't returned. Besides, we are not here to please Stella Adams. The larger purpose is Wakanda's relationship to No Nation Left Behind and all the good they plan to do around the world. If we ourselves cannot help other countries, then we can partner with an organization that can. It is good for public relations."

"Public relations," Okoye says under her breath as her thoughts travel back to Brownsville, and she wonders if her king would think of doing any good there *for public relations.*

King T'Chaka remains diplomatic, noble, and genuinely kind during more meetings, a lunch, cocktails, a dinner, more cocktails, and modeling for Okoye and Captain Aneka how Wakanda should be perceived in the outside world. When they finally end the day in their hotel rooms, exhausted and uninspired, King T'Chaka goes off into his penthouse suite while Aneka and Okoye share a large bedroom with double king-sized beds.

Dora Milaje are trained to abstain from having too much leisure time, but getting adequate sleep is a top priority in order to do their job. In just a few minutes, both Okoye and Aneka are dressed for bed. Except Okoye is wide-awake and the captain is as still as stone beneath her covers.

Quietly, Okoye gets out of bed and rummages through her suitcase for something comfortable. Luckily, she and Aneka brought workout clothes. Part of the Dora Milaje disciplinary code is to exercise regularly. In Wakanda, the state-of-the-art Upanga Training Facility along with the outdoors, wide-open space, and fresh air are where they practice their combat techniques. But here, Aneka told Okoye that they will have to work out in a gym, a fraction of the space they are used to in Wakanda.

Black leggings, an *I Love New York* T-shirt that Captain Aneka had brought her from her last trip here, a hooded sweatshirt, and tennis shoes are as close to her Dora Milaje tunic as she will get. She slips on her Kimoyo bead bracelet, knowing that the captain will find her if she needs her, and folds her spear into the sleeve of her shirt. Her Dora Milaje spear is the size of her palm and can extend to her height when she needs it. She grabs the useless phone she and the captain were told to carry as a formality. The king has one, too, so as to look as if Wakanda is up-to-date with their technology. "So primitive," Okoye whispers to herself as she moves swiftly and quietly, and in no time she is waiting outside the hotel trying to hail a taxi. If she gets reprimanded, she will have to suffer the consequences without any complaints.

Okoye stands at the edge of the sidewalk holding her hand out like she sees so many other New Yorkers do. But none of the taxis stop for her. Several pass her and stop for passengers who weren't even hailing a cab. She imagines holding up a spear to threaten a taxi driver to stop. But that would be a bad idea since they all seem to be afraid of her for one reason or another. Just a few feet from her, a couple holds up their hands, too. So Okoye drops her hand and steps back. Within seconds a taxi stops for the couple. The man opens the back door and grabs the woman by the waist, and they begin to kiss good-bye. Okoye steals her chance. Like a swift leopard, she darts toward the taxi and leaps into the backseat, slamming the door shut behind her.

"Ey, I did not stop for you!" the taxi driver exclaims with a thick foreign accent that Okoye recognizes as either Nigerian or Ghanaian.

"Brother, why do you discriminate?" Okoye asks as the couple starts to bang on the passenger-side window.

"You people don't tip!" the taxi driver says.

"You people?" Okoye repeats. "How dare you? I am from Wakanda. *My people* will give you one hundred times your tip!" Okoye reaches into the pocket of her hoodie, pulls out a wad of cash, and throws it onto the passenger seat of the taxi.

The driver looks over at the cash, shifts the car into drive, and speeds away from the curb as the couple continues to protest.

The drive from Midtown to the edge of Brownsville is quick, but not without some observations from Okoye. The neighborhoods in this city are like different countries. The borders are both invisible and as clear as daylight. Whatever riches New York City has are not equally distributed throughout all the corners of this place. While one place is thriving like the lush Congo River Basin, another part is barren and dry like the Sahara Desert. Still, that is nature's doing. But here, it is the people who do this to each other, Okoye realizes. And it's not fair.

"This is as far as I will go," the taxi driver says, stopping the car at the end of a tree-lined block.

"Is this Brownsville?" Okoye asks, despite already knowing the answer to that question because she can see the red air in the far distance, like a force field. Hot air, Tree called it. They've stopped at what appears to be the edge of that red bubble, and it's clear that the driver had taken the safer streets to get here.

"Of course not. It's the middle of the night and I have a family to return home to."

"What are you afraid of, my brother? The people who live there are just like you and me."

"Miss, I've heard stories of taxi drivers dropping off customers and then a ball of flame flies above their car. And I don't know what will ever possess me to burn down my own neighborhood. Besides, that red air is toxic. No telling what that's all about."

"So you see it, too?" Okoye asks.

"Everybody sees it. But seeing it and doing anything about it are two different things. You know, see no evil, speak no evil. And if anybody else asks, I don't see nothing and I don't know nothing."

"Then you must know about PyroBliss."

The taxi driver quickly clutches the wheel and says, "Thank you for riding with us, ma'am."

"Haven't I paid you enough? Maybe I should take back . . ."

The driver pulls a few bills from out of the wad and tosses the rest back to Okoye. "No, you have not paid me enough."

He refuses to drive any farther or answer any of Okoye's questions. Not willing to push the issue, Okoye darts out of the taxi and braces herself for the walk to Brownsville.

After several blocks where the brownstone buildings are pristine, flower boxes hang from windows, and young people sit on the front stoops, Brownsville's visible border is closer, redder, hotter even. She walks through it waiting to feel its energy, but there's only a warm sensation against her skin as if she's stepped out into the sun. At the end of the block, Okoye spots them. She can tell by their dark silhouettes beneath the streetlights that these are the kids who protect Brownsville like an army. But Okoye wonders who their leaders are. Who are their true warriors?

"You again?" a boy asks. "I see you're trying to dress like a New Yorker now. Nice try, but you still look like a tourist. Welcome to Brownsville." He stands with his legs spread apart and his arms crossed, wearing a thick black jacket, too thick for such warm weather, and gray sweatpants.

"Yes, me again," Okoye says. She walks closer to the boy with his head cocked back as if ready to challenge Okoye. "At ease, child."

"Child? We're like the same age."

"She's not from around here, remember?" Tree comes out of the shadows and her friends part, making a path for her as she walks toward Okoye. Her hair is pulled back into several long braids adorned with gold-and-silver metal beads. Her denim jacket is slung over her shoulders and a gold pendant in the shape of a tree hangs from a thin gold chain around her neck.

Tree and Okoye stand face-to-face, neither saying a word.

Then Okoye steps back, gives Tree a once-over, and says, "PyroBliss."

"What about it?"

"You tell me. It seems to be a problem here. Is it why this place you call home is so . . . broken?"

Okoye catches a girl nudging Tree. They all start to step back.

The girl steps forward. She's a bit shorter than Tree, stocky with a head full of thick, curly hair. A septum ring and dark red lips let Okoye know that she's a tough one. But she recognizes her as the girl the group was hiding the other day. The one they had formed a semicircle around: Mars. The one who Lucinda described as being *strung out*. "Look, sis," she says with a deeper, raspier voice. "I don't know what you and Lucinda got going on, but it's too late to be paying her a visit anyway.

And we don't know about that pyro whatever. We're just out here chilling."

"I am Okoye. Nice to meet you," Okoye says.

"Mars. Mars Cooper."

"I already know."

"Then run and tell whoever sent you. Now go and mind your own business," she says.

But as soon as an SUV with blacked-out windows approaches them, the kids move toward it. The truck stops and a backseat window rolls down just as the trunk pops open. Mars quickly runs over to grab a big green duffel bag from out of the trunk and closes it. The kids step away from the SUV as the window rolls up, and it starts to drive off.

Okoye remembers what Lucinda told her about Stella Adams. She and her husband are responsible for bringing PyroBliss into Brownsville. But how? In a duffel bag?

"Nonsense," Okoye whispers to herself. Then she calls out, "Ey!" and starts running toward the vehicle.

She picks up speed, but her sneakers are useless compared to her Dora Milaje combat boots, which are designed specifically to give her a little more boost. Nonetheless, Okoye can run in anything and on any terrain, so she is getting closer to the SUV even as it turns a sharp corner. It picks up speed and runs a red light. Another car is approaching the intersection. It is about to hit Okoye, but she thinks quickly, even as her heart races, and she leaps over the car so high and with such force that when she lands, she feels her bones and organs rattle. She breaks her fall with both hands and one knee on the ground. Okoye pauses to quickly grab a Kimoyo bead from her bracelet and holds it in the palm of her hand to survey her body for any injuries or broken bones. The bead sends waves throughout her body, and she feels the tingling sensation on her skin. The result is negative. She is fine. She discreetly snaps the bead back onto the bracelet.

The SUV is gone, and Okoye immediately worries that she has done too much. She has shown too much of her true self here in Brownsville, so far from Wakanda.

"Yo! Did you just straight up jump over that car?" a voice calls out in the distance.

Slowly, Okoye gets up and wipes herself down. She turns to see Tree, Mars, and their crew running toward her with their mouths agape and eyes wide. She thinks of something to divert the attention away from what they might have just seen. "Where is the bag?" she asks.

"Hold up, girl. You don't get to ask the questions. We do. Who are you really, and why are you here?" Tree

e don't own any of those buildings, except
la's community center. Maybe when it all burns
we can build everything back up and finally get to
l of it," Mars says as she herself walks toward the
. "Now mind your own business, girl!"

oye has never taken orders from someone other
Captain Aneka, the Dora Milaje headmistress, or
ng. Why should she be so obedient to this child?
does not move one inch as she watches the flames
distance followed by cheers. "This isn't right," she
ers to herself. "There is too much suffering here."
ou better get out of here," Tree says as the small
walks past her and turns in to the dark alley. "We
need you to save us."

r a moment, Okoye is frozen where she stands.
this girl is right. Captain Aneka would certainly
so. The king would reprimand her for being this
om him on a trip like this. What is she supposed
now? Go back to the fancy hotel, slip under her
comfortable covers, and go to sleep? Rest while
ng there are places like this where children are
ng down their own homes and enjoying it? But as
da had told her, this isn't their fault. Maybe this
liss is like the heart-shaped herb. But the heart-
d herb doesn't have power *over* the Black Panther;
sn't make him do anything. It only enhances his

asks. "And why in the world did you run after that car
like that? Who do you think you are?"

They are all panting and out of breath.

Okoye blinks and bites her bottom lip. She will be
honest. "I am from Wakanda. I am a member of the
Dora Milaje, a special group of women trained and
charged with keeping our king safe."

Tree steps forward. "We get that you're from
Wakanda and all, and that y'all are supermodel bodyguards or whatever. But *you're* supposed to keep the king
safe? It's like me being part of the president's secret service or something. That doesn't make any sense."

"Besides, Wakanda is poor, with nothing but ele-
phants, giraffes, grass, and mountains," a boy in the
group says.

"Hmph," Okoye says. "I do not think they teach you
the truth about Wakanda in your schools, or about anywhere in Africa for that matter. Now, who was in that
big car?"

"If you don't know who was in that car, then why
were you chasing it?" Tree asks.

Okoye looks around at the small crowd of kids, who
are all staring at her suspiciously. The group is smaller
now, and in the distance, Okoye spots Mars turning a
corner into a dark alley. "I think it was Stella Adams."

The kids all shift—some exhale, some cross their arms, some move their weight from one foot to the other. Okoye's question has touched a raw nerve with them.

"It's okay, y'all," Tree says to her friends. "She already knows." Then she turns to Okoye, licks her lips, and says, "She does real estate and runs this big company. But she's not coming all the way out here. Can't you see gentrification hasn't reached this part of Brooklyn yet? And are you also some kind of undercover cop for the United Nations or something? What's with the questions?"

"Gentrification?" Okoye asks. "Is that a drug like PyroBliss?"

The kids laugh, but Tree holds up her hand to make them stop. "You know what? I guess you can say that," she says. "Gentrification is when a neighborhood doesn't get the help that it needs from the government, and things fall apart until people with more money and resources start to move in."

"But isn't that a good thing?"

"No!" all the kids say as they shake their heads, clearly even more impatient with Okoye. Tree continues, "When they move in, we're pushed out. They don't want us around here when things start getting nice."

"I see," Okoye says. "It's like co[...] and all over the world."

"Exactly!" Tree says.

"But how can you stop this [...] Okoye asks, as she remembers the [...] independence all over Africa she [...] schoolgirl and while she was traini[...] Milaje.

But before Tree can respond, [...] distance—laughing and shouting.

And then a booming sound ca[...] and cover her ears, an instinct th[...] been allowed to determine her first [...] lasts for a moment before she's off ru[...] and toward the smoke and fire.

"No! Stay out of it!" Someone su[...] front of her, forcing her to stop. It's [...] spread apart with her arms crossed.

"Move. Or you will be moved," O[...]

"Who do you think you are? B[...] hero?" Mars says.

"There is a fire. People are gettin[...]

"No, people are not getting hu[...] want to watch it all burn."

"This is your home. Why?" Okoy[...]

powerful abilities. Besides, it is a plant grown from Wakandan soil, not created in a lab or a factory like many other things in Wakanda. What power is PyroBliss enhancing in these young people while they are burning down their own homes? What power do they gain when they do this? And according to Lucinda, there is one person to blame for PyroBliss: Stella Adams.

Okoye's feet make the decision for her. She starts walking toward the flames and sees the kids in the distance on Rockaway Avenue. In an instant, Okoye is at their heels and they don't notice that she's right behind them. Mars leads the group to a dumpster before reaching behind it and pulling out the duffel bag.

Okoye quickly hides behind a parked car as Mars passes the bag to Tree, who takes the lead as they walk into a gated apartment complex guarded by two tall, muscular men. The kids are buzzed in, and the gate quickly opens and slams shut behind them. The apartment complex looks brand-new compared to the burned-out and dilapidated buildings around it. Okoye wonders why and how this place is protected compared to the rest of Brownsville. So she starts to make her way toward the guards and the gate. And there it is. The huge sign spells out in white letters PRIVATE PROPERTY. NNLB.

The two men immediately turn to face Okoye without saying a word.

"I'm here to see Tree and Mars," Okoye says calmly.

One of the men cocks his head to the side. So Okoye does the same.

"They're not distributing until midnight," he says with an unusually soft voice.

Okoye looks up at one of the buildings and notices someone staring out of a window. "Stella sent me. I'm checking in," she lies.

The other guard nods and slowly walks to the gate to press a nearby button. They wait for a buzz. Nothing.

"They don't know I'm coming. Orders from the king. I mean, the boss," Okoye lies again. The guilt of having to do this is burning at her core. But she must get past this security to see what this distribution at midnight is all about.

As soon as the gate buzzes, Okoye darts in and runs toward the nearest building, where someone pokes their head out of a window to call out, "Hey! She's not supposed to be in here!"

No matter. Okoye is much faster than those two guards could ever be. She's already observed that the window is on the fourth floor and has made it through the front door and darted up eight flights of stairs, only to be greeted by several closed and locked doors to apartments.

But it's Tree who opens one of the doors and says,

"Clearly you can't mind your own business. You want answers? Fine. We got questions, too." Tree holds up her hand to the guards as they rush out of a nearby elevator. She motions for only one of them to come toward her and points to Okoye.

"Do what you must," Okoye says, lifting both arms over her head.

The guard pats her down and takes Okoye's phone from her pocket, handing it to Tree with a nod.

Okoye walks into the apartment, and Tree slams the door shut behind her.

CHAPTER 8

The apartment is nearly empty, and there are no adults around. Okoye walks around slowly, noticing the shiny marble floors beneath her feet. She's on guard, as if someone will jump from behind a hidden door to attack her at any moment. But all she sees are the faces of these children. They stare at her with a mix of fear and curiosity disguised as aggression.

"Where is your family?" Okoye asks.

"Our family is at home. And don't look at us like we're a bunch of stereotypes because of what you see going on outside. We have homes and people who love us. This is just somewhere we can kick back and chill. Now stand down, soldier. Nobody's gonna come for you in here," Tree says, handing Okoye's phone back to her.

"I will stand down only when you surrender," Okoye says, taking her phone.

"We're not surrendering to nobody. Now unlock your phone."

Okoye does as she's told, knowing that she has nothing to hide. If going through her phone will ease some of this girl's suspicions, so be it. "This war of yours . . . you think you will always win? You think that you can never be defeated?"

The kids look at one another and then back at Okoye. Tree motions for one of the men to pat her down again. Okoye holds up her hand. "No need. You must think there is only one type of weapon."

"Stop with the riddles," Tree says, giving Okoye back her phone once again. "Who are Captain Aneka and King T'Chaka? They're your only contacts. A *captain* and a *king*? The ones you came here with the other day?"

"Yes, you've already met them. And I like to believe that I am welcome when I visit the home of a friend. Please, disarm yourselves of these tough exteriors. How about a smile for your guest?" Okoye says with her own smile, remembering what King T'Chaka has told her about charm and wit.

Tree rolls her eyes and the others sigh. "You don't

get it, do you? O-ko-ye, or whatever your name is, you're going too far by coming up in here and you're lucky that I didn't let those guards handle you."

"Handle me? Ey! They are the ones who are lucky," Okoye says. "Now what is this place?"

"No, we ask *you* questions. Not the other way around." Mars comes out from another room at the far end of a hallway.

"Since you will not answer my questions, then I will look for the answers myself," Okoye says, and starts to walk around the apartment.

There is a single black leather couch and a few floor pillows. A giant flat-screen TV takes up most of the wall space in the living room, which is adjacent to a state-of-the-art kitchen complete with stainless-steel appliances and marble countertops. It's a stark contrast to the crumbling neighborhood outside.

"Welcome to the crib, Black She-Hulk," Tree says. "You've figured out a way to get all up in our business. Make yourself comfortable because you're not leaving until you tell us what you want from us."

"Are you selling PyroBliss out of this apartment?" Okoye asks without hesitation.

There are six kids in total. Two boys take a seat on the couch—a short, chubby one with slick hair, and a tall, muscular one. One sneers at her. The other pulls a phone out of his pocket and starts to play a game. "She gotta go," he mumbles.

"Where is the bag?" Okoye asks. "Why is Stella Adams making you do this?"

"Is she serious?" a girl asks, and steps closer to Tree as if telling her to do something.

Mars throws something at Okoye, and she quickly catches it with both arms. "Is this what you're looking for?" Mars asks.

It's the duffel bag. Okoye holds the bag and stares at both Mars and Tree. But Tree only glares at Mars.

"What are you doing?" Tree says through clenched teeth.

"There's enough PyroBliss in there to set the whole world on fire," Mars says to Okoye. "You want it? You can have it. Take it back to Wakanda and see what happens."

"I will not do such a thing. I will destroy this," Okoye says.

Tree's eyes widen, but Mars laughs. "We'll just say you stole it from us. But they're not even gonna mess with you. At least not right away."

"So they will come for you?" Okoye says. "Even if I try to run out of here with this bag, you are the ones who will pay the price? And who should I expect to come knocking on my door when they are through with you? Stella Adams?"

"If you want answers to those questions, all you have to do is run out of here with that bag," Mars says. "Let's see you try to take that to Wakanda. It's probably part of the plan, anyway, and you should know this if you're working for her."

"Mars, what are you doing?" Tree demands again, stepping closer to her girlfriend so she's staring directly at her. "We'll all get in trouble!"

Before Okoye can say another word, there's a knock on the front door. Then another, louder this time.

"Open up!" a woman's voice shouts from outside the apartment.

"You have to give that bag back!" Tree whispers. "If you're really trying to help us, then you have to get out of here. Hide somewhere!"

Okoye drops the duffel bag and quickly scans the apartment. She spots a set of sliding glass doors on the other side of the living room. She rushes to it, steps out onto a balcony, and hides behind a wall just as someone pushes open the front door. Okoye peeks around the wall and she sees her. Stella Adams is standing behind a few muscular men: her goons. They step aside and allow her to enter the apartment first. Okoye glances at all the kids' faces. Their eyes are wide, mouths slightly open, and their bodies are frozen where they are. This woman clearly has a lot of control over them. Stella's eyes dart about looking for something or someone, so Okoye ducks behind the wall again. The sliding doors are still open, and it'll be seconds before Stella decides to poke her head out.

Okoye can't let Stella find her here. Not just because the kids will be reprimanded in some way, but because it may get back to the king, or even worse, Captain Aneka. She may not be sent on any more special assignments. Whatever allyship the king has formed with Stella will be ruined, regardless of whatever plans she has here in Brownsville. Most importantly, Captain Aneka will lose confidence in Okoye as well, and it may jeopardize other Dora Milaje's chances of traveling to America. Here she is, worlds away from home, putting her life in danger, and it's not even for the king. She's also putting the lives of those kids in danger if Stella finds her here.

The balcony is small and narrow, but there is enough room for her to step away from the window and wait until Stella leaves. Okoye hears Stella's voice coming closer.

"I've gotten word that you've had a visitor," she says.

"Yeah, there was this lady snooping around, but we took care of her," Mars quickly says.

"Oh, did you?" Stella asks.

"She just wanted to help us poor, troubled kids, that's all," Tree adds. "We told her we're good."

"Is that so?" Stella says. Her voice is much closer now, as if she's standing right by the sliding doors.

There is a stack of bricks on the balcony, maybe some leftover construction supplies from when this building was being built. Okoye notices an ember sparking on one of the bricks. She wants to put it out, but doing so would make her visible to Stella.

"You don't have to do that, Stella," Okoye hears Tree say. "We don't want none of that red smoke to come into the apartment."

"Oh, just practicing. That's all," Stella says. "And besides, you're used to that red air."

And in the blink of her eyes, the stack of bricks explodes, sending a gush of hot air toward Okoye's face. Blue-orange flames lick at her legs, and it's bound to spread all over the balcony.

Luckily, all the floors in the building have balconies, so Okoye quickly calculates the distance between this balcony and the one below before she leaps over the rail and swings from the ledge, landing on some fake grass and nearly knocking over a potted plant. She spots a couple through the sliding glass doors. They're different from everyone around here. They're white, and Okoye doesn't remember seeing any colonizers in Brownsville, but there two of them are, in a beautifully furnished apartment whose walls are covered with artwork and shelves of books.

One of them quickly turns around, and Okoye leaps over the rail of that balcony and then the one below, until she lands at ground level. The entrance to the building is around a corner, and several men are guarding the front doors. Okoye quickly ducks behind a dumpster and eases her way out of the complex, crawling, leaping, dodging, and running until she is out of Brownsville, riding on the number 3 train back to Midtown Manhattan, panting, sweating, and with such an adrenaline rush, she feels ready to fight a war.

Captain Aneka is standing in the middle of the hotel room with her arms crossed when Okoye tiptoes in. Okoye freezes, letting the door slam shut behind her. "I went for a run," Okoye says. "I see this is what the New Yorkers like to do. They run to nowhere at all hours of the night."

"And you ended up in Brownsville again?" Aneka says firmly, holding a Kimoyo bead in her palm. "You are being dishonest to my face."

Okoye inhales and looks away. She doesn't say

anything; instead, she starts to change out of her running outfit.

"Okoye, please," Aneka says. "I do not want there to be any distrust between us."

Okoye sits on her bed and exhales. "They are only a couple of years younger than us, Captain. Do you remember us at sixteen? Light in our eyes, so full of potential."

"We were young, but we did not have our heads in the clouds," Aneka says.

"Yes, we were tough and strong but still young. We were Dora Milaje before we even knew what it meant. But we had time to be . . . *children*."

Aneka sits beside Okoye. "Those children you were telling me about . . . is this what you saw in them?"

They are doing things they should not be doing simply because they have no other choice. The PyroBliss controls their minds."

Aneka exhales. "This is the case all around the world, Okoye. You mustn't allow your heart to become so attached."

"But we are not all around the world. We are here in America, New York City, one of the wealthiest places on earth."

Captain Aneka stands to look down at Okoye. "You have to stay away. Yes, it is all right to be concerned, but we are not duty bound to help those children. Wakanda is our duty. King T'Chaka is our duty. Let it go, Okoye. It doesn't seem that you will be catching up on rest. We might as well get ready for tomorrow's meetings."

"Will we be meeting with Stella Adams?"

Aneka inhales. "She has a luncheon planned."

"Tree and Mars could be me and you had we come into this world under different circumstances," Okoye says, staring intensely at a painting on a wall.

"You have to stay away, Okoye. You are compromising not only yourself, but the safety of the king and your position as a Dora Milaje when you sneak out into the night like that. If you meddle any further, you could be exposing what Wakanda truly is to the rest of the world. I hope you haven't promised those children anything, Okoye."

"Tell me, Captain. What is Stella Adams compromising by visiting those children in Brownsville? Why was she in their apartment? What is she exposing by being there?"

Aneka steps closer to Okoye once again. "Whatever it is, the risks for her are different. It isn't any of our concern. Stella has been nothing but cordial and welcoming to our king. That is what matters most now."

"Am I supposed to look away when something terrible is happening to those children and their village?"

"Village? There are no villages here, Okoye. Only . . . I don't know . . . colonized places. If I could help you help them in any way, I would. But we are not in Wakanda. Soon we will be returning home and all our attention will be needed there."

"Colonized places, eh? I guess here, the colonizers never left. They colonize over and over again. Not like in Africa, where the people celebrate independence every year, right? What independence do they have here, eh, Captain? They are not free. Their homes are being destroyed to build tall, shiny buildings in the middle of ruins. Ruins, Aneka. They call it gentrification. Tree told me all about it. And those colonizers are helping the people, *our* people, burn their own homes to the ground." Okoye says this in almost one breath. She holds her head down as if she's said too much. These words were lodged in her throat, and it's a relief to finally get them out. But she knows there isn't anything her captain can do.

"You sound as if you care very much, Okoye" is all Captain Aneka says.

"I do, and you should've briefed me on the history of these places. We become like the colonizers when we visit countries, cities, and even neighborhoods without knowing the full truth of who the residents are." Okoye pulls up her sleeve, taps a Kimoyo bead on her bracelet, and it begins to pulse and glow. "Search history of Brownsville and Stella Adams," Okoye says into the bead. A voice responds:

Compiling data. Accessing historical database from the New York Public Library. Search complete.

In seconds, the bead projects a hologram of swirling red smoke before it gives way to a black-and-white city landscape that reaches from the floor to the ceiling of the hotel room. The image zooms in until both Okoye and Aneka recognize the streets of Brownsville. But something is off. The streets are the same, but the buildings are different—old architecture yet clean and new. The smaller and narrower street signs with the rounded edges let them know that this is the past, and the streetlights are more like tall vintage lamps. There are people, but not like the ones they've seen in Brownsville.

"Colonizers!" Okoye exclaims.

The hologram zooms even farther in on a building where a little girl jumps rope alone. She is wearing a dress and lace socks. Above her, an old woman wearing a handkerchief pokes her head out. "Estelle!" the woman calls out. Her voice is faint in the video.

"Coming, Grandma!" the little girl replies, and she drops her rope on the ground just as a man walks toward her. She runs to him and he picks her up, holding her tight.

"Papa!" the little girl sings.

The man puts her down and holds her hand as they walk into the building together. The old woman looks out onto the streets as she waves to passersby. A mailbox next to the building's front door reads *The Adamskis*.

The hologram image speeds up as if being fast-forwarded. The white people start to disappear one by one as people of different races start to appear. Some with light brown skin and long, dark, curly hair. Children play on the streets just as people hide in corners and sleep on cardboard, seemingly swallowed by an invisible sadness. Soon there are more Black people like the ones in Wakanda. As the people change, so do the buildings. They become weathered and broken. The hologram slows again to zoom in on an empty lot where the girl and building had been. A car pulls up, and out of the backseat a blond woman emerges—Stella.

The hologram retreats back into the bead.

"That is her? Stella Adams," Okoye whispers.

"No," the captain says. "It appears as if Stella Adams is named for her—a grandmother, perhaps. The signs, the cars, the clothes all reveal that this was many, many years ago. Brownsville was home to Stella's family. The community center stands where her family home used to be."

"So of course she would want to take over, no matter who lives there now. She is trying to hold on to what she thinks is hers."

"No matter. This does not concern us, Okoye," Aneka says. "Promise me you will not interfere. What if something happens to the king and you are off gallivanting in Brownsville, eh? It's clear that Stella has an interest in Brownsville, and I need you to stay out of her way. I need you here. Wakanda needs you to be with your king."

"I know, I know." Okoye stands from the bed and holds her head up, remembering that she is Dora Milaje first and foremost. Duty calls, and that duty is to her king and her nation. She must try to push all that she's learned about Tree, Mars, and Brownsville out of her mind. Her training has taught her to stay focused on the moment, to be alert, and not dream up what could or should have been in a potential utopia. Okoye has seen the beauty of Brownsville in the faces of the people and in the art that covers the still-standing walls. She hears it in the music and the language. The true Brownsville exists beneath the layers of hurt and suffering, beneath the rubble, and even buried deep like flowering seeds that promise to bloom one day in sunlight, if only someone would remove the heavy, dark, smoky clouds. Or better yet, that thick red air.

Okoye's and Aneka's phones vibrate. It's certainly the king, so they both rush to see if he's in any kind of trouble, wondering why he would not use a Kimoyo bead instead. But only the words *Good night, Dora Milaje* appear on the screen.

Captain Aneka chuckles. "We can't let these primitive devices collect dust while we have them. They must be good for something. Okoye, send a text to the king as a formality."

When Okoye picks up her phone, she notices that a new contact has been added to her very short list. Tree Foster is her most recent contact. She must've added it when she took the phone from Okoye. Okoye quickly responds to the king with simply *Good night, Your Highness.*

Then in a new message, she types, *I cannot have you as a contact on this phone. I am sorry, Tree Foster. I will not be disturbing you and your friends in Brownsville anymore. Be well.* Okoye sends this text to Tree and waits in the bathroom for her to respond. It will be closure between her and Brownsville once and for all. But Tree does not answer.

Morning comes and Okoye checks her phone again. Nothing from Tree.

"Are you expecting a message from the king?" Aneka asks. "You should check your Kimoyo bead."

"No," Okoye says, hesitantly deleting the sent message and Tree from her contact list. Something settles in the pit of her stomach. Tree put her number in her phone for a reason. But Okoye can't risk her captain or the king seeing this name in her phone. They will have too many questions for which she will not have answers. Still, why didn't Tree respond to her text? No matter. It's over. Tree, Mars, and Lucinda Tate were living their lives before her arrival to New York City, and they will continue to live their lives long after she's gone. Whatever fate awaits them, it is none of her business. This is what Okoye tells herself so that she can finally get some peace of mind here in New York City, worlds away, it seems, from home in Wakanda.

Late into the night, a Kimoyo bead vibrates on Okoye's bracelet. The red-orange glow lets her know that Ayo is trying to reach her. Not wanting to disturb her captain as she sleeps, Okoye tiptoes into the bathroom. She places the bead on the counter and a hologram of Ayo appears as she smiles big and bright.

"Sister!" Okoye sings.

"I wasn't sure I would reach you," Ayo says. "I know

it is the middle of the night in New York City, but it is early morning in Wakanda."

"It is so good to see you, Ayo!"

"Okoye, you have been misbehaving?"

"Who me? Misbehaving? Where did you get that news?" Okoye asks, knowing that the captain and Ayo have been communicating.

"We Dora Milaje are connected in more ways than you know, Okoye."

"Ayo, neither you nor the captain prepared me for this trip. I am seeing and learning things I could not have imagined."

"I remember my trip very well. Please, Okoye, know that you have been prepared. There is so much about the world that not even a Kimoyo bead can reveal to us. We have to go see for ourselves. There are wars big and small that we are prepared to fight. But not all battles belong to us."

"If you say that we are prepared, then we should fight all battles. There are people who are losing every war. Why mustn't we help them?"

"Because we are not an army for the world. There are too many sides to choose."

"The place is called Brownsville, and it is not the world. It is a neighborhood in Brooklyn and I wanted to help the people who live there, but Captain Aneka has convinced me that it is not any of my concern. I am needed for Wakanda and Wakanda only."

"She is right. And you were also right to want to help. Okoye, we are also Wakanda. Wakanda exists because of us. So wherever we go, we take Wakanda with us, all of it. Your war, be it internal or external, is our war."

Static appears on the hologram, and Ayo's image becomes fuzzy. Okoye taps the bead to cut off the transmission just as her captain knocks on the bathroom door.

CHAPTER 9

"**P**lease, Captain Aneka and Okoye," King T'Chaka says as they approach a conference room on the top floor of a high-rise building the next morning. "If you could stand guard outside the meeting room, I would greatly appreciate it. I was told this was a private meeting and by invitation only."

"My king, we cannot leave you alone in there," Aneka says.

"At the very least, let us take a look at the conference room," Okoye says. At last, this is something that requires her attention. A private meeting? The king wants them to not be by his side? What could this be about?

Okoye steps into the conference room and spots

a giant screen displaying the No Nation Left Behind Industries logo. In front of the screen are pamphlets with photos of children playing outside of tall, sparkling buildings. It all looks like just another meeting to Okoye, but she can't shake the nagging feeling that this is more than that. There's no proof here, only her Dora Milaje instincts. "Everything is all clear, my king," Okoye says when she's out of the conference room.

"Thank you, Okoye. I hope you understand that I have to respect the rules of my hosts. There are secrets I have to keep for the security of our nation, and the safety of others, I'm sure Captain Aneka has explained to you such matters. However, if there is anything that will directly impact my safety or Wakanda's, you will certainly know about it," the king says as he starts to step away from Aneka and Okoye.

"Even if it's not about Wakanda, will you tell us?" Okoye asks. Captain Aneka shoots her a look and the king furrows his brow.

"No, I will not," King T'Chaka says. "I also have a duty to my guests here. I would like to be invited back, you know. But trust me, if it is anything that endangers Wakanda, you will know before the words leave my mouth."

Out of the corner of her eye, Okoye spots Stella Adams walking toward them. The blond woman doesn't acknowledge her, even as she slides her hand across King T'Chaka's shoulder and kisses him on the cheek. The king is taken aback by the gesture. "Ah, Stella, lovely to see you. You know, I must tell you that I am eager for you to meet my wife, Queen Ramonda."

"Good morning, Your Highness," Stella says. "I would love to meet her and I am sure she is a lovely queen. And I've heard about your late wife, N'Yami. . . . I know I am a few years too late, but I am sorry for your loss."

Okoye clenches her jaw. Aneka widens her eyes at her.

"Ladies." Stella nods at Okoye and Aneka.

"Good morning, Ms. Adams," Aneka says. Okoye remains silent.

"I hope you both had a restful night. I hear those hotel room sheets feel as if they've been made from baby's breath. So incredibly soft, don't you think?"

Okoye locks eyes with Stella, but she is the first to look away. She made a promise to her captain and to herself, as well as to the king and to Wakanda. She will leave unimportant matters alone. None of this has anything to do with Wakanda.

King T'Chaka and Stella walk away toward the conference room doors. Other guests start to arrive, and the lobby is abuzz with chatter. A small group of kids, teenagers like Tree and Mars, walk into the lobby. They are dressed in suits and skirts and are looking around as if they've never been in a building like this before.

Okoye motions for Captain Aneka to take a look at them. "Too young to be diplomats, don't you think?"

Aneka only furrows her brow and keeps her eyes on the kids. There are six of them, and their faces are lit up with bright smiles and clear eyes. Okoye scans them, hoping to see anyone familiar, but she's never seen them before—not in Brownsville, not on the trains. Of course, New York City is a big place. There are millions of young people, but why would any one of them be at a private meeting for No Nation Left Behind Industries?

A girl walks up to both Okoye and Aneka and holds out her hand. "Hello. You two must be representatives from Wakanda," the girl says, smiling, revealing a set of braces. Her long braids hang over a bright yellow blazer.

Neither Okoye nor Aneka takes her hand. "How did you know that?" Aneka asks.

The girl points to a pin on Okoye's lapel, something Okoye had not noticed until now. Okoye smiles. "Ah, yes, you are familiar with the Wakandan flag?"

"I know all the countries in Africa," the girl says.

"And what is your business here?" Aneka asks.

"I have an apprenticeship with NNLB. We all do. I work for Ms. Adams."

Okoye inhales just as Aneka glances back at her.

"What is it that you do for Ms. Adams?" Okoye asks.

"Lily!" someone calls out. Stella is standing in the entrance to the conference room as she calls the girl over.

"I gotta go, but I want to learn more about Wakanda. Maybe visit to help the poor kids read or something. Like how Ms. Adams is helping the ones in Brownsville. So maybe I'll see you again one day. Nice meeting you!" the girl says cheerfully, and rushes toward Stella.

"Don't even think about it," Aneka says through clenched teeth.

"Think about what?"

"Don't go meddling in things that have nothing to do with Wakanda. Remember your promise, Okoye."

Okoye inhales and tries to push the thought from her mind: Why does Stella have all these children working for her? She has them in Brownsville and now more are here at this secret meeting. And how is she helping those "poor" children?

"Maybe I should go check on the king," Okoye says, thinking that she may be able to peek into the conference room.

"If he needs us, he knows where we are," Aneka says.

Captain Aneka is right, Okoye realizes. He may need them for something. As a Dora Milaje, she has to be present and alert, always. It's as if Okoye turns off one switch to turn on another. She stands tall beside the conference room doors, politely smiling at passersby and nodding when spoken to, but she allows Aneka to do the small talk. She's still not sure whether she is a fashion model or just a bodyguard now, but she holds her position and doesn't let her mind wander to other places and people.

Two hours go by before the conference room doors finally open and a small crowd of people begin to rush out. Okoye glances into the room, where the screen with the NNLB logo now also displays the words *A Tree Grows in Brownsville*. She's seen those words before on Lucinda Tate's T-shirt. Okoye's mind begins to race. If Stella has something to do with whatever Lucinda is doing in Brownsville, then why wasn't she at the ribbon-cutting celebration?

Okoye spots Stella out of the corner of her eye. The kids surround her and it looks as if she is giving them a pep talk. Okoye starts to walk closer, but the king's voice forces her to stop and pivot toward him.

"Yes, Your Highness," Okoye says.

"Where are you going?"

"Those children . . . they are so endearing. I wanted to finish a conversation I started with one of them. Lily, I think her name is," Okoye says.

King T'Chaka steps closer to her, and the captain is right behind him. "Ah, yes. They are the most precocious young people I have ever met. I didn't know they had a hand in building that community center we visited in Brownsville. So dishonest of that woman to take all the credit. What was her name?"

Okoye raises her brows and Aneka comes around to face the king, but she silently cautions Okoye to not take this conversation any further.

But Okoye says, "Her name is Lucinda Tate. Did Ms. Adams mention her at this meeting?"

"I am glad that the meeting was informative, Your Highness," Aneka interjects. "Shall we head back to our rooms for some rest before the next event?"

"You two go ahead. I will stay back and finish a chat with Ms. Adams," King T'Chaka says.

Okoye and Aneka exchange looks. "My king, what is the purpose of this chat with Ms. Adams?" Okoye asks without hesitation.

"She would like me to learn more about NNLB's plans to expand to other nations. It's clear that Wakanda is on her radar. I can at least hear what she has to say, but do not worry. I will be listening with two sets of ears if she is speaking out of both sides of her mouth, as they say. If she speaks with two mouths, I will have four ears to understand."

"I think Queen Ramonda would love to hear your voice. Shall we ring her when you are finished with your chat?" Okoye says.

"Yes, that would be nice," the king says.

"My king, we will wait for you here. I prefer that we be by your side," Aneka adds.

"Very well, then. And please alert the queen that I will be phoning her later this afternoon."

King T'Chaka walks away and Okoye exhales. "Captain, how are you keeping your suspicions at bay? You do have suspicions about that woman, don't you?"

"Of course. But all we can do is watch and remain alert. Our king is not a fool, Okoye."

"I believe that Ms. Adams thinks he is," Okoye says.

Aneka doesn't respond and steps away from Okoye as if she is returning to her post. But there are no posts here. Okoye and Aneka do not have assigned locations at which to stand and wait for orders from the king. Nonetheless, no matter how many times Aneka jokes that they are supermodels from Wakanda, their Dora Milaje instincts are always beneath the surface of these false exteriors. The captain is acting on her instincts just as much as Okoye is acting on hers. Or is she? Was it her Dora Milaje instincts that allowed her to feel a pull back to Brownsville? Or was it something else? Still, Okoye stands by as well, keeping her attention focused on the king, even as Stella Adams continues to throw herself at him.

Stella glances at Okoye and Aneka and motions for the king to follow her back into the conference room. The doors shut. Okoye starts to make her way to the conference room without looking back at Aneka, who would certainly protest, but before she takes another step, her phone vibrates and she immediately knows that it's Tree.

We need your help, the text message reads. *Mars got hurt.*

Okoye doesn't spend too much time questioning her new position as a super hero for these kids. They called her for help and there is nothing else to do but show up. Even the king will understand this need to serve and protect, and maybe Aneka will not protest her leaving in the middle of yet another event to go help these kids. But Okoye does not explain. She simply says, "I will be back," and takes an elevator down to the lobby, where she walks out of the building to hail a cab to Brownsville.

CHAPTER 10

"You are not afraid to drop me off here?" Okoye asks as the driver eases into Brownsville and stops in front of the apartment complex.

"Afraid of what?" he says with a big smile. "These are my people. Why would I be afraid of them? They're just seeing some tough times, that's all. I'm sure it's the same thing wherever you're from. But you know what? We always rise above the dark clouds. Ain't that right?"

"Yes, you are right," Okoye says, a bit taken aback by the driver's optimism. Before Okoye even steps out of the cab, a guard rushes to open the door for her. The guards make room for her to pass through the gates leading into the apartment complex. The other night, she had to sneak her way out of here. Now she is a welcome guest because of Mars.

A boy is standing by the door to the building wearing a jean jacket and a green baseball cap. Okoye recognizes him from the apartment the other night. He motions for her to follow him. Soon they are in an elevator where the boy is quiet with his headphones on, bopping to the beat of his music. The elevator doors open, and Tree is standing there with her arms crossed over her chest and her brow furrowed as if she is carrying the weight of the world.

Tree uncrosses her arms and exhales. "Thanks," she mumbles.

"Where is she?" Okoye asks.

Tree rushes to the apartment with Okoye at her heels. As soon as the front door swings open, Okoye sees Mars lying across the black leather couch. She isn't bleeding and her clothes are intact, but she is unconscious. Her face is wound up as if whatever has put her under must have been very painful.

Okoye does not need to ask what happened. The details never matter. The life and soul of the person comes first. Instinctively, she reaches for her Kimoyo bracelet hidden beneath the sleeve of her shirt. But Tree is peeking over her shoulder. There are five others standing around, some biting their nails, some pacing, others staring at Okoye as if she is about to perform a miracle. She is, but they mustn't know.

Okoye eases one of the beads into the palm of her hand. Then she places her hand over Mars's forehead, allowing the bead to rest there for a moment, glowing and vibrating while the warmth penetrates Mars's head. A bolt of electricity stings Okoye's hand, and in an instant, Mars begins to cough, but she doesn't wake up. Okoye quickly places the bead back onto her bracelet.

"What'd you do?" Tree asks, rushing over to hug her friend.

"The curse broke," Okoye says.

"Curse? How'd you know it was a curse?" Tree asks.

Okoye's eyes meet Tree's. "She was not moving. What else could it be?"

The mood in the apartment shifts as the kids start joking and talking among themselves.

"Look, you're not bringing that African mumbo jumbo up in here," Tree says. "Nobody is putting curses on anybody. She just . . . got into a fight, that's all."

"You do not think a fight is a curse? A curse results from ill intentions. Someone wanted to hurt her. Who was trying to hurt her? Did she take PyroBliss?" Okoye asks.

"You and this PyroBliss," Tree says, shaking her

head. "When you were here, you said you wanted to help, so we wanted to see what you could do."

Okoye goes over to Mars and takes her hand. "She needs to see a doctor. I am a warrior."

"Who is this lady, anyway?" asks one of the boys who is standing around. He's tall and gangly but with a commanding presence.

A hard knock on the door causes everyone to jump, except Okoye, who leaps toward the door with such speed, everyone's eyes widen. "Whoa!" someone says. "Is she for real?"

Another series of knocks. "Did somebody call nine-one-one?" a woman's voice says from the other side of the door.

The kids all shake their heads. "We don't usually open for the police," Tree whispers.

But Okoye ignores her and opens the door. "But the guards let them in for a reason. What is nine-one-one, anyway?"

A man and woman dressed in paramedic uniforms stand in the hallway with a gurney behind them. "Is everything all right? We got a call that someone was hurt in this apartment," the woman says.

"Nah, we're good," one of the boys says.

"No, no, they are not good," Okoye says, opening the door wider. "Her name is Mars and she needs a healer."

"No. She did not just answer the door," one of the other girls says.

"What planet are you from, lady?" another says.

"We said we're good," Tree says, stepping closer to the front door.

"Ma'am, are you the only one of legal age here?" the paramedic asks Okoye.

Okoye looks around at the kids, who seem to all be disappointed in her. But she is here to help and that is exactly what she intends to do. "Yes, I am the adult."

"Did you call nine-one-one?"

"No, she didn't," Tree says. "And she's not in charge of us, so y'all can leave now."

Okoye takes another look at Mars, who is not moving. She knows that whatever is hurting her is internal. There isn't anything else Okoye can do without revealing too much about the science of the Kimoyo beads. "Please, her name is Mars and she is not waking up," Okoye says, and lets the paramedics in.

Tree glares at Okoye with such ferocity that she is sure that it's a hex. Mars is quickly and gently placed on the gurney and the paramedics rush her out. Okoye, Tree, and the other kids take the stairs and meet behind the ambulance as the paramedics load Mars in.

"Naya," Tree says to another girl. "Go with her, I can't."

"I can go," Okoye says.

"No, Naya is her sister. She's family," she says, then lowers her voice. "They'll ask you too many questions."

Naya climbs into the back of the ambulance, the doors shut, and the ambulance drives away as its lights flash and the sirens sound, echoing throughout the block and the entire neighborhood.

It grates on Okoye's ears, but she realizes that blaring sirens are common in Brownsville. People keep getting hurt here as if they are doing hard labor on farms or shepherding cattle. Someone always needs help.

Tree steps closer to Okoye and says, "We called *you* for help, not them."

"Tell me who did this to her, and I will help," Okoye says.

Tree shakes her head. "You really didn't have to come. You don't have to try to save us," she says.

"Did Stella Adams do this?" Okoye asks.

"She knows you were here. Whatever you two got going on, my girlfriend paid the price for it," Tree says, lowering her voice.

"I did not tell her anything."

"Did you see who was following you? Don't you know that when you get within an inch of Stella Adams, she'll come sniffing around herself?"

"I know who she is and why she is so interested in that community center. There used to be a building there, and it was where her mother grew up. She wants to take it back. She wants to take all of Brownsville back. I see signs of her everywhere here," Okoye says.

"What do you mean she wants to take it back?" Tree shouts. "Is that what she told you? Well, guess what? It wasn't hers in the first place. My mother grew up here, too. And my grandmother moved to this neighborhood probably when Stella and her people got the heck up out of here."

"Why did you ask me to come? What did you think I could do about Mars?" Everyone has dispersed, and they are standing beneath a dim streetlight as more sirens wail in the distance. There's a chill in the air, and Okoye only feels it on her head and legs since she is still wearing her blazer, skirt, and heels from today's meetings. But Tree only has on a T-shirt and jeans, and Okoye notices the goose bumps on her deep brown skin.

Tree turns around and steps closer to Okoye. "Lucinda Tate told us that you and your friends were on a humanitarian mission," she says. "You were attending conferences and meetings to learn how you can help people around the world. Well, Brownsville is the world. We need a humanitarian mission here."

Okoye exhales, both surprised and relieved by what Tree is saying. "That is why I asked you all those questions. I wanted to know. If I don't know anything about you and the people here, then I won't know how to help."

"I saw the text you sent. You said you wouldn't be coming around here anymore."

"I . . . I have other duties."

"Yeah, I get it. Africa is more important. Poor kids in other countries are more important. We got ambulances and police here, so we're good, right? All we gotta dial is three numbers, nine-one-one, and all our problems go away." Tree takes several steps back, turns around, and starts to walk away.

Okoye chases after her and stops right in front of her. "That is not what I think, Tree. I am from a different place. I can only go by what I see. So you have to let me know how I can help. Is it the PyroBliss? Is it Stella Adams or something much worse?"

"So you don't learn about America the same way we don't learn about Africa?"

Okoye is taken aback by that question. She doesn't have an answer for Tree.

"Facts" is all Tree says, and walks away.

Okoye doesn't chase after her. She's been defeated. She replays the last few minutes in her mind. What if she hadn't let in those healers—paramedics, they called them? What if she'd used more Kimoyo beads on Mars and held them against her head and heart much longer for the healing science to take effect? Surely she would've woken up. But Tree would've asked questions that Okoye could not possibly have answered. Or what if she'd never answered the call in the first place? What would have happened to Mars?

Okoye takes the slow and long way back to the subway station. She passes Lucinda Tate's office, but it's dark and empty. She passes people standing on corners, eyeing her suspiciously. She passes entire families, it seems, huddled together against buildings and on sheets of cardboard with all their belongings piled into rusty shopping carts. Smoke rises in the distance and a few more buildings appear to have been burned down since the last time she'd been here. Tree was right. There is nothing she can do here. If this place is broken because of PyroBliss, then how can she get rid of the drug by herself? If PyroBliss exists because of Stella Adams, then how can Okoye stop her all by herself? More questions flood her mind as she enters the subway station. There are police around, so she doesn't want to risk being reprimanded, or whatever they do to people who break the laws here, for jumping the turnstile. She taps a Kimoyo bead instead and holds it near the turnstile.

Okoye rides the subway, replaying all of the day's events in her mind as she is taken farther and farther away from the brokenness.

CHAPTER 11

Both Okoye and Captain Aneka memorized the king's schedule before arriving in New York City. There was no need for daily planners or reminders. The phones were only a formality so as to appear like the rest of the world: plugged in and logged on. So Okoye knows she has fifteen minutes to change out of her suit and into a dress for yet another formal event—this time a Broadway play.

A sinking feeling settles in her belly. Captain Aneka may have already checked her Kimoyo bead to see where she is. Okoye will have to tell the truth, and she will have to ask for help. She braces herself to lay out everything to her captain exactly how she had witnessed it. Whether or not it was wise to get the king involved would have to be up to both Okoye and Aneka. Okoye inhales as she gets closer to the elevators, summoning the bravery and integrity of the Dora Milaje to tell the truth.

The elaborate double doors to the elevator open to reveal none other than King T'Chaka. Okoye's heart skips a beat. She holds her breath for a long second before saying, "My king. Good afternoon."

King T'Chaka steps out of the elevator with Captain Aneka right behind him. "Good *evening*, Okoye."

"Right. *Evening*." Okoye glances at Aneka, who wears an apologetic look on her face.

I tried, Captain Aneka mouths.

"May I ask why my two guards were separated from each other?" King T'Chaka asks. "Captain Aneka greeted me outside my meeting with Stella unaccompanied by you, Okoye. What is the reason for this?"

Okoye drops her head, not out of guilt but out of respect for her king. And she cannot lie. "My king. I returned to Brownsville."

King T'Chaka exhales, disappointment settling on his face. "You have not been communicating with me, Okoye. You did not use a Kimoyo bead or alert Captain Aneka of where you were going."

"I apologize for my negligence, my king," Okoye says.

"We don't have time to sit and discuss. Let us walk and talk," the king says.

Okoye, Aneka, and King T'Chaka leave the hotel and wait for their limo.

"So what is this obsession with Brownsville, eh, Okoye?" he continues.

"My king, if you had seen what I've seen, your heart would go out to the people of Brownsville, too," Okoye says.

"Well, we have been there, and it seems as if Stella Adams will be cleaning up the mess that Lucinda Tate started. I saw it all in the slide presentation during today's conference."

The limo arrives and the driver comes around to open the rear door for them. He's a short, stocky man who seems oblivious to who they are.

"No, there is more beneath the surface, King," Okoye continues when they're all seated inside the limo. "Stella Adams is not telling the truth. Lucinda Tate is trying to do her very best for the children of Brownsville, but there are more sinister, more powerful forces trying to stop her."

"Okoye," Aneka interrupts. "Why don't you come out and say what you need to say?"

Okoye exhales and says, glancing at the driver and lowering her voice, "My king, it is my suspicion that

Stella Adams and No Nation Left Behind Industries are exploiting the people of Brownsville. She is causing more harm than good."

"Ah, nonsense, Okoye. What proof do you have?" King T'Chaka says.

"She was there. I saw her visiting with some of the kids who were part of the marching band we'd seen. One of them was hurt today, and Stella Adams had something to do with it. But that is only the beginning."

"Go on."

"And there is something called PyroBliss—" Okoye suddenly stops speaking because Aneka taps her leg. She doesn't even glance over at her captain to realize that they've made a huge mistake. Okoye pauses and she immediately senses why Aneka stopped her. The driver is listening to them closely.

"Ah, yes. Ms. Adams shared some information about it. Something about fires and . . . it makes people do terrible things," King T'Chaka says. "But Ms. Adams, her husband, and NNLB are all trying to help clean up places like Brownsville. We shouldn't get in their way."

"You do not understand, my king," Okoye says, whispering now. "Cleaning up means something different to them. Their idea of dirt is not our idea of dirt."

"Okoye, as king of Wakanda, I have seen all kinds

of cleaning up around the world where people who look like us are considered garbage. I have seen the worst in human beings, and I have also seen the very best," the king whispers. "Whatever it is that you think Ms. Adams and NNLB are up to, you should stay out of the way."

Okoye doesn't say anything else for fear that something will get back to Stella. Surely she has spies everywhere. Okoye remembers what Tree told her about getting within inches of Stella and the reach her goons have. Maybe this driver is one of her goons. Maybe they are all over the hotel lobby, and they report back to Stella when Okoye leaves and when she arrives. Maybe this is why Stella sent a message to the kids via Mars.

The car drives down Broadway, where the lights are flashing, advertisements and commercials appear on huge screens, and the streets are crowded with tourists and pedestrians. The weight of everything she's experienced in the past few days starts to settle on Okoye. There is so much of *everything* here in this place called Times Square: shining lights, fancy things, busy people. In Wakanda, everyone has enough, and there is enough for everyone. Why can't a little bit of all these riches here trickle down to Brownsville?

The car pulls up in front of a theater where a long,

velvety red carpet extends from the front door to the edge of the sidewalk. A man wearing a suit reaches out toward the limo to open the door for King T'Chaka, then Captain Aneka, then Okoye. Before stepping out of the limo, Okoye glances at the driver, who's been staring at her in the rearview mirror. His face is calm, but he narrows his eyes at Okoye, then forces a smile. Okoye doesn't smile back. She eases out of the car with a deep suspicion stirring in her belly.

Okoye and the captain follow the king into an empty and quiet corner of the theater's lobby. They all look around. No one is paying attention to them as more theatergoers arrive and the lobby begins to fill with people they haven't seen before. Here and now, they can be invisible for a moment.

"My point is, Okoye," King T'Chaka says, continuing where he'd left off. "There are many instances where I wish I could gather all of Wakanda's riches—toss out a handful of Kimoyo beads, slip some of our technology into the hands of a healer—but that would be a major transgression against the throne, the elders, and the people of Wakanda. We have seen what has happened all over Africa with outsiders coming to take and take, leaving us with nothing but famine, drought, bloodshed, corruption, and greed."

"I understand, my king," Okoye says, swallowing hard. The king is not telling her what she needs to hear. How does he just look away? How does he not feel the pull to help? There must be something, with help from a Kimoyo bead, that would enable a noble-hearted Wakandan to do the right thing.

"And I understand you, Okoye. It is quite admirable of you to want to help. This lets me know that you are a righteous Dora Milaje with a kind heart and a warrior spirit. But this must end now. I should not have to repeat how this puts everyone—*everyone*—in danger." The king's voice is stern now, a tone he uses only when he feels it's absolutely necessary. King T'Chaka is indeed a noble king. But that nobility extends only to Wakanda, and not his brothers and sisters in other nations—those who look like Wakandans.

But what kind of injustices has King T'Chaka witnessed in other parts of the world? Surely he's aware of the destruction from war, the abuse of children. These are the results of corrupt governments, greed, and general misfortune. In none of those instances, perhaps, was the king in close proximity to anyone who was causing these injustices. Or maybe the king has shaken hands with instigators of war many times over. Still, if Stella Adams is responsible for PyroBliss and Mars getting hurt, then the king should do something about it, especially if she is constantly smiling in his face and inviting him into private meetings.

T'Chaka and Captain Aneka begin to make their way into the theater and she spots Stella Adams in the distance waving the king over.

"My king," Okoye says softly so no one else can hear. "You have not seen what I have seen."

The king glances over at Stella in a way that lets Okoye know that maybe he is already aware of what she is capable of. The king is wise, of course. He knows that the people of Brownsville, and maybe other parts of the world through No Nation Left Behind Industries, will suffer at the hands of Stella Adams.

"This ends now, Okoye. And this is the very last time I will address the matter," King T'Chaka says, even more sternly this time.

Aneka blinks at Okoye, a nonverbal way of letting her know that she sympathizes with her, but under the orders of their king, she has to obey.

Stella tries to take the king's arm when they greet each other, but King T'Chaka gently pulls away. In that moment, Okoye realizes that knowing is not enough. Awareness of injustice means nothing if there isn't any action to effect change. This is what she feels in her gut. She is not a king. She is not a politician nor a diplomat. She is a Dora Milaje, protector of the throne of Wakanda. As close as Stella Adams is trying to get to the king, maybe protecting the people of Brownsville is also protecting the king from whatever sinister plan she has for him. And she definitely has a plan. Okoye is sure of it. But Okoye's hands are tied. She has no choice in the matter.

Okoye follows the crowd into the theater and finds a seat next to Aneka. She feels so out of place here with the plush seating and elaborate art covering the ceilings. They are a few rows from the stage and Okoye looks around to see that there are many kinds of people in their part of the theater, except ones that look like them. Though the king did not mention it, she suspects these tickets were a gift from Stella. She knows that the king is getting special treatment in exchange for a favor. But what could that favor be? There is nothing else to do but to sit back, stand by, observe, and protect. Okoye can hardly enjoy the show, which is a hip-hop opera in which all the cast is dressed in clothes from a faraway time and a long-ago place. Her mind races back to Brownsville, Tree, and Mars. The pull is stronger now, but she is stuck here watching a show performed by actors who could be those same kids. A different road has led them here, and Okoye wonders why all the kids in the world are not traveling that same road—a road that could possibly lead them to a stage where the audience celebrates their talents and gifts with a standing ovation.

Okoye and Captain Aneka settle down for the evening by watching the news. This is indeed a vacation because they've never been so inactive since they became part of the Dora Milaje. Back in Wakanda, there is very little leisure time for the Dora. Each free moment is for exercise and to recharge. They don't call it rest. They call it fueling. Food is fuel. Sleep is fuel. So what purpose does it serve to sit on the edge of a bed watching other people tell you what to think and what to do?

"Why are we watching this nonsense, Captain?" Okoye asks.

"This nonsense is information. Don't you want to learn more about America? Even what they consider to be humorous and fun is quite fascinating," Aneka says.

"I feel as if I am losing brain cells just watching this."

"What did I tell you, Okoye? You mustn't be so judgmental. Simply observe. You will learn a lot more just by paying attention to what is going on without any kind of agenda."

"Or what they tell you is going on," Okoye says, after watching a few minutes of the news in which there was no mention of Brownsville or PyroBliss. She's seen what they don't want people to believe is happening in America.

"Let's practice some combat moves instead, Captain," Okoye says. "We can have this on in the background."

Aneka agrees, and she pulls out her Vibranium spear, rotates her wrist, and it extends out to almost twice her height. Luckily, the ceilings in their hotel room are high enough for Aneka to maneuver the spear around her hand. Okoye gets into position as well. She simply holds out her arm, and her spear extends out from her sleeve in a horizontal position, almost knocking over a nearby floor lamp. They will have to be careful, but the need to hold a spear in their hands and get into a friendly battle is much too strong for them to care about any damage to the furniture.

Aneka is the first to swing, and the music from a commercial on the TV is the perfect soundtrack to their jabbing, retreating, blocking, and spinning. Okoye and Aneka are equals in combat, so this practice will have to involve one allowing the other to win. No matter. It's good exercise, especially when all they have to do is stand by their king all day. They have to do the same in Wakanda, thankfully. But here, Okoye can't help but feel the pervasive threat to the king's safety. Not his physical safety—his intelligence is being undermined.

Stella is playing him for a fool. This is not the sort of threat that requires combat. But nonetheless, these few minutes of practice allow both Okoye and Aneka to keep their minds sharp.

The pointed head of Aneka's spear nearly grazes Okoye's cheek. She dodges to her left just in time. Aneka freezes, holding the spear with both hands, narrowing her eyes. Then she exhales after she realizes what she'd almost done.

"Your guard is down, Okoye," Aneka says. "Your mind is much too preoccupied. You do not need to explain what is troubling you."

Just as she says this, Okoye hears Stella Adams's name on the TV. Her face shows up as she is standing in front of a building with a giant red bow stuck to its shiny new double doors. Okoye flicks her wrist and her spear disappears into her sleeve. The captain does the same as they both step closer to the television screen.

"Cofounder and CEO of No Nation Left Behind Industries celebrated her nineteenth ribbon-cutting ceremony today in Newark, New Jersey," the newscaster says. Then the camera switches to a video of Stella giving a speech before a crowd in front of the building. A sign is now visible on the screen and it reads: A TREE GROWS IN NEWARK.

"What an honor to be able to serve the people of

Newark. It has always been the mission of No Nation Left Behind Industries to include American cities as part of its humanitarian mission around the globe. No Nation Left Behind also means that we don't leave Americans behind in our global pursuit of health, wealth, and equality for all. I am proud to launch the grand opening of this community center and affordable-housing complex for Newark's most vulnerable population. This is No Nation Left Behind's nineteenth community center in major cities across the United States. Next stop, Brownsville, Brooklyn—a community that is truly in need and will now be afforded a state-of-the-art center that will serve as a safe haven and resource for its community members. Please join us this weekend in Brownsville to celebrate NNLB's twentieth venture, in Brooklyn's forgotten neighborhood." Stella is all smiles with her slick bun and bright red pantsuit. The audience cheers and applauds.

The camera pans out to the surrounding buildings in Newark, and Okoye immediately recognizes buildings that are dilapidated and burned-out just like the ones in Brownsville. The crowd there is a mix of what looks like businesspeople and politicians with a few local residents sprinkled in. Okoye is sure that most of the people of Newark are not attending this ribbon-cutting celebration.

"Something is not quite right with this picture," Okoye says aloud.

"But it appears as if she is doing a lot of good in these places," Aneka says.

"If that is the case, where are the people? How come they are not by her side?" Okoye asks. The person who cuts the ribbon is the little girl who had approached her at the conference the other day: Lily. "We met her," Okoye says, wondering if she is a resident of Newark.

"Okoye, will this be the same building we visited in Brownsville that Stella is cutting the ribbon for next, or another building?" Aneka asks.

"I don't think it matters," Okoye says. "I think they want to take over the whole place, so one building will be no different than the other."

Their New York trip is almost coming to an end. Okoye hasn't been able to shake off this sinking feeling that she has done something terribly wrong. King T'Chaka and Captain Aneka notice that something is weighing heavy on her mind.

"As soon as we board the plane back to Wakanda, you will leave all that is troubling you behind," King T'Chaka says. "That is what I always do when I visit places that could use Wakanda's help, but I cannot offer any sort of assistance. I do my best, Okoye. Our humanitarian visits are not in vain. You will be surprised at how far a few words of wisdom can go in a country that is desperate for some direction. That is all that we can offer—words that instill kindness, hope, and healing for the broken parts of our world. The world knows that Wakanda is a peaceful nation. Yes, they think we are poor, but we are also humble and . . ."

"We mind our business," Captain Aneka says, finishing King T'Chaka's thought.

King T'Chaka has been invited to attend an NNLB press conference in Brownsville in front of the same building to which Lucinda Tate had invited them. The questions swirl around Okoye's mind, but she's made a promise to the king, and there are only a few more days until they return to Wakanda. What does NNLB hope to achieve in Brownsville, anyway? Okoye has been checking her phone frequently, even sending a text to Tree asking how Mars is doing, but she's gotten no reply. She is worried about her new friends, and she doesn't want them to think that she's abandoned them completely. But she has to erase them from her mind and her heart. And yes, she has to mind her business, even though she is certain she will see them today.

Okoye will have to pretend as if those few days in Brownsville did not happen while she's in the presence of the king and the captain, even though she's told them about her visits. It is to protect her heart. Or else, saying good-bye to those kids will be that much harder, Okoye plans to stay vigilant and inexpressive while at the news conference. She wonders if Tree and Mars will finally have the opportunity to perform in that marching band. She also wonders if all the TV news crews will bring more attention to what is happening in Brownsville, and then the world will know what is really unfolding in other places like it, including Newark.

But how will they know Stella's true intentions?

No Nation Left Behind Industries has sent a car to pick up the king, Okoye, and Captain Aneka. Okoye is doing what she's been doing these past few days—her head is up, eyes wandering and attentive, and her mind is narrowly focused on her duties.

But when she sees Lucinda Tate standing outside the hotel, she lets her guard down and she knows right in that moment that their trip is far from over.

CHAPTER 12

"Ah, Ms. Tate!" King T'Chaka sings, genuinely delighted to see her. "What brings you here to Midtown?"

Okoye immediately notices the look of worry on Lucinda's face, and she knows that something is not right.

"Good morning, Your Highness," Lucinda says, smiling politely at the king, and she nods at Captain Aneka. But her eyes are steady on Okoye, as if to say she's here to see her and only her. "Okoye, can I talk to you for a sec?"

"My king," Okoye asks, "may I step away?"

The king politely nods as Okoye and Lucinda step

aside. King T'Chaka and Aneka wait at the curb for their car.

"How is Mars?" Okoye asks immediately.

"Mars is fine now, but . . . things are getting worse, Okoye. For one, I lost the building," Lucinda says. "My money has dried up and I couldn't get any investors to help furnish the place and pay for programming, except, of course, your friends."

"My friends?" Okoye asks.

Lucinda glances back at the king. "Let me guess. More fancy cocktail parties, brunches and dinners, the theater, and your own private car? It's from Stella, isn't it? She and NNLB are the 'friends' I'm talking about."

"It's politics and diplomacy," Okoye says, trying to reassure Lucinda that she is not one of Stella's beneficiaries.

A black car pulls up to the curb. "Okoye," King T'Chaka calls out, eyeing her suspiciously.

Under any other circumstance, Okoye would not wait one second to heed her king's call. "Go on," she whispers to Lucinda while nodding to her king, assuring him that she'll be there in a second.

"Look, I know you were with them the other night—Tree, Mars, and their crew," Lucinda continues. "That apartment you were in, they got kicked out. She changed the locks and everything. It was just a place to hang out as part of a deal with Stella. They got to chill in a nice apartment while they worked for her, Okoye. And now . . ."

Out of the corner of her eye, Okoye sees Captain Aneka holding the rear door open for her. King T'Chaka is already in the car. "Come with us," Okoye says.

"In Stella's car? Absolutely not. I don't want to be anywhere near that woman. That's where the press conference is. She'll be announcing that she's taking over as manager and all those sponsors that I was supposed to get, they'll be knocking on her door. She and NNLB were the only ones who promised to help with the upkeep of the building and getting in those computers and furniture that we desperately needed. But instead of just helping, she took over, claiming that I couldn't do it alone. She basically pushed me out of my own project. I've worked so hard on that community center."

Okoye glances back at Aneka one more time, swallows hard, and says, "Is there anything I can do?"

"That's why I'm here, Okoye. Look, this is not about the building. This is about the kids. I've watched Tree and Mars grow up here. They're bright kids with big dreams. Stella got into Mars's head, and . . ." Lucinda sighs. "It's not good. She's destroying their futures, their lives. If there's anything you can do—"

Aneka clears her throat loudly. Okoye looks back and she instinctively starts to step away from Lucinda. As a Dora Milaje, her body has been trained to do what it's supposed to do, regardless of what her heart and mind tell her.

"I understand," Lucinda says, and walks away.

"Meet me over there," Okoye whispers after her.

But Lucinda doesn't turn around. At the very least, they are both headed in the same direction. Okoye will have to see for herself the turmoil Lucinda referred to in Brownsville.

"So, Stella has taken over this building, eh? And now she wants the world to know by having a press conference. I suppose that by taking over this community center she thinks she is the ruler of Brownsville?" King T'Chaka says to Captain Aneka as the limousine eases into Brownsville. The streets look no different than any other regular day, with people walking in and out of stores, sitting on stoops, and going about their business. It looks the same as the day they were invited by Lucinda when she was hosting the launch of the community center.

But Stella Adams had promised a private celebration after her press conference, like the one Okoye had seen on the news. Newark had been bustling with people celebrating and cheering. But here, there are no politicians, no children whom Okoye recognized from the conference room, and certainly no local residents. What was so different about Brownsville?

As the car approaches the community center, where there isn't even a big red ribbon tied in front of the entrance's double doors, a line of guards emerges from seemingly out of nowhere.

"What is this?" Okoye immediately asks the driver.

"Protection," he says.

"Protection for whom? The king is safe with us."

"Don't you mean *from* whom?" the driver asks.

An armed and uniformed guard opens the car's door, and Okoye is the first to jump out to survey the streets and the building. "What is going on?" she asks the guard.

"Ma'am, please quietly make your way inside the building."

"Not until you tell us what is the meaning of this," Okoye says. "We were invited here by Stella Adams for a news conference."

"Ms. Adams would like to see you inside," the guard says.

Okoye glances around and no one seems to notice or care that their car is parked in front of this brand-new yet empty building. She doesn't recognize any of the very few passersby, and in that moment, she desperately wants to contact Tree to find out if she knows anything about what's supposed to happen here. Something is stirring deep in her belly, and she trusts her instincts.

"Okoye, is it safe for the king to exit from the vehicle?" Captain Aneka asks from inside the car.

"Yes. Let us go," Okoye says, and in seconds, she, Aneka, and King T'Chaka are walking through the set of sliding doors leading into the building that is supposed to be a community center for the people of Brownsville.

A wide and brightly lit hallway opens up into a rotunda with sparkling marble floors and a glass ceiling. Much like the apartment buildings where Tree and Mars had set up shop for the PyroBliss serum, this place is a stark contrast to all the other buildings in Brownsville. Okoye can't help but wonder if the rest of Brownsville will soon look like this—a new city built on top of ashes and memory.

High heels clicking against the floors is the only sound Okoye hears in this vast, empty space. Within seconds, Stella Adams appears and following close behind her are Mars and a few others from her crew.

"Ah! So lovely for you to finally join us," Stella sings.

Okoye discreetly gives Mars a once-over, trying to

see if she's been hurt in any way. But from the looks of it, Mars is wearing brand-new clothes and sneakers and looks much better than the last time Okoye had seen her. Relieved that Mars is relatively well, Okoye glares at Stella suspiciously. "What is going on here?" she asks, wanting to avoid all niceties. "There was supposed to be a press conference."

"Yes, very much like the one for Lucinda's failed attempt at a ribbon-cutting celebration. These people have scared away the press, and since there will be no press, there won't be a conference."

"Ms. Adams," King T'Chaka interrupts, "I'm sure there is a reasonable explanation for the lack of festivities today. However, our time here is coming to an end, and I'd like to make the most of the rest of our stay in this fine city. What is it that we can do for you and the people of Brownsville?"

"Better yet, what have you done *to* the people of Brownsville?" Okoye asks, glancing at Mars, who stands back with her arms crossed as if guarding whatever decision she's made to be here.

Stella extends both her arms out and spins. "Can't you see? This, my friends, is what I have done for the people of Brownsville!" she sings.

Okoye wants to speak, but Captain Aneka gently touches her arm, reminding her to stay in her place.

"But what about Lucinda Tate?" King T'Chaka asks, taking the words right out of Okoye's lips.

"Oh, please," Stella says, looking back at Mars. "That woman would've let this building burn to the ground, just like everything else around here. She can't control those addicts."

"Addicts?" King T'Chaka asks.

"I'm sorry. Did I say addicts? I meant *children*." Stella walks over to Mars and places an arm around her. "King T'Chaka, I would like you to meet Mars Cooper, the head of my new youth task force here in Brownsville. I was inspired by your own guards, the Dora Milaje, as you call them, to employ some of the young women in this neighborhood. Give them something to do with their time. I wish I'd had something like the Dora Milaje when I was growing up as a teen in New York City. I know what it's like to have all this misplaced rage and fighting spirit. Isn't that right, Mars? Anyway, with the help of a few of my new guards sprinkled about, Mars here will keep those kids in check. She is now Captain Cooper!" Stella gives her a sharp salute.

But Mars nods in agreement without saying a word and without even looking in Okoye's direction.

"Pleased to meet you again, Mars Cooper. Or Captain Cooper. I remember you from the marching band," King T'Chaka says.

"Yes," Okoye interjects. "You and your girlfriend, Tree."

"Ah, Tree Foster. So you two have met," Stella says. "I thought so. Too bad you didn't get wind of how that miscreant ruined all our plans for today's news conference."

Okoye's ears perk up and she meets Captain Aneka's eyes, but she holds back on saying anything else that would reveal her friendship with both Tree and Mars.

"So there is someone to blame?" King T'Chaka asks.

"A whole slew of them, King," Stella says as she walks around Mars and the others. Her heels click even louder, as if each step is deliberate. "They think they run this neighborhood. All the adults here seem to have given up on them. No boundaries, no discipline. Don't you see how they are burning down their own homes?"

PyroBliss echoes in Okoye's mind, but she doesn't dare say this aloud. Stella is blaming the kids, but it's the drug that makes them do these things. Okoye wants to show the world the truth, but this is not the time or the place.

"Is that so, Mars?" King T'Chaka asks, and Okoye is relieved that her beloved king is taking the initiative to get to the truth.

"Um, yeah," Mars says without hesitating. "They're

not listening to Lucinda Tate. They don't trust her because she said she was going to get all these sponsors to get some furniture, equipment, and computers for this community center, but she bailed out on us. Ms. Adams came to save the day."

"You believe that? Because I do not think that is true," Okoye interjects.

"Yeah, why wouldn't I? You know something I don't?" Mars says, glaring into Okoye's eyes as if daring her to spill their secret.

Okoye has been to the apartment where both Mars and Tree were hiding the bag of PyroBliss. She'd seen Mars strung out on the serum. She saw Stella with her own two eyes come into that apartment and threaten those kids. But saying all this would put Tree and all the others in danger. What would that mean for Mars, who clearly has already sided with Stella? A hint of doubt flashes across Okoye's mind. Was Mars forced to be here?

Okoye inches closer to King T'Chaka and whispers, "Maybe Mars should give us a tour of the place. See what Wakanda can do for the people of Brownsville?"

King T'Chaka steps away from Okoye, places his hands behind his back, and walks around the rotunda examining the art on the walls, the floor-to-ceiling windows, and the many tall, fake plants. "I'm so sorry

we did not get to officially open up this beautiful building to the people of Brownsville. You've created nothing
short of a regal palace here, Ms. Adams," the king says.

Okoye hears a hint of sarcasm in the king's voice.
The structures in Wakanda are far more beautiful and
sophisticated than this.

"Lucinda did most of this," Mars interjects.

Okoye smiles a little, happy to hear that Mars is getting to the truth.

"But she didn't finish. What sense does it make to
have a beautiful building if it will stay empty and collect
dust? Stella is finishing what she started."

"Is that the truth?" Okoye says.

But Stella steps closer to the king and pulls him
away from his guards, taking Okoye's attention away
from Mars. "You like?" she asks.

"Very much," King T'Chaka says. "What other
surprises do you have lurking here? Would you mind
giving us a tour?"

"Well, as you know, No Nation Left Behind
Industries is replicating these community centers all
over the world. In places as close as Brownsville and as
far as, say, Wakanda." Stella smiles wide and glances at
Okoye and Captain Aneka.

King T'Chaka chuckles. "No Nation Left Behind
Industries in Wakanda? That would be something. But

I do not think we've been left behind, Ms. Adams. We are very much where we are supposed to be."

"Oh, you people are so humble. You refuse to accept any help from the outside world. That's why I think NNLB and Wakanda would be a great partnership. Humanity and humility go hand in hand, don't you think, Your Highness?"

Okoye and Aneka exchange looks again. It's clearer now why Stella Adams has been cozying up to the king.

"What do you think, Aneka and Okoye? The children in Wakanda would find a place like this so magical. I'm sure they don't have anything like a community center over there," Stella says, stepping closer to the Dora Milaje.

"You are correct. They do not have anything that even comes close to a place like this. How about that tour, Ms. Adams? We would love to see how opulent this place is," Okoye says through clenched teeth. Wakanda's centers are far more technologically advanced and are much more functional than this pretentious display of vapid wealth, but Stella Adams can't know this.

Stella cocks her head to the side and smiles insincerely. "We have to respond to the people's demands and protests. They've put themselves in a tough position. Investors don't want to pour money into this community center if it is headed by Lucinda Tate. Of course, they would rather someone from that community run it, but someone more agreeable, willing to bend a little. However, I refuse to simply be a silent investor. NNLB is the face of any and every project we sponsor. We want the world to know about the good we are doing in every corner of this city and, hopefully with your help, King T'Chaka, in every corner of this world. On the bright side, there is a fabulous, state-of-the-art auditorium on the top floor. I have invited the press to meet us up there. No need to add to any of the commotion in this neighborhood. The guests will arrive shortly and Mars can take you up there, where waiters will greet you with cocktails and hors d'oeuvres. Enjoy! King T'Chaka, I'd like to continue giving you a private tour of the place. Do you mind?"

"Not at all, Ms. Adams," the king says before he walks away with Stella, nodding toward Okoye and Aneka as if to say that he will be all right. He quickly taps his wrist, letting them know that if he needs them, he will contact them through a Kimoyo bead.

The captain and Okoye nod, obeying the king's secret orders.

"More cocktails?" Aneka whispers to Okoye.

Okoye chuckles, glad that they'll have some private time with Mars. But they are led out of the rotunda by the entire crew, all seven of them. As soon as Okoye and Captain Aneka are out of Stella's and the king's sight, Okoye turns to Mars. "How are you doing?" she asks.

"I'm good. You?" Mars says, only glancing back at Okoye as she presses a button between two shiny elevator doors.

"You were hurt and you were sent to the hospital."

"I don't know what you're talking about."

"Mars, I . . ." Okoye stops midsentence when she feels Captain Aneka's hand on her arm.

Aneka gestures toward a camera near the ceiling. The elevator doors open and only four of the crew step in, leaving the rest behind. Both Okoye and Aneka look around for any cameras in the elevator. Okoye spots one in the corner. She steps closer to it, looking directly into the lens. She reaches up, grabs it, and in one swift pull, she yanks it out of the elevator's wall.

"Whoa!" Mars calls out. "What'd you do that for?"

"You think they are watching you?" Okoye says. "Are you afraid?"

"Yo, who *are* you people?" Mars asks.

"We have a few seconds. Are you forced to be here?"

"Nah, I'm good. I'm here 'cause I want to be."

The elevator doors open to an auditorium much like the theater they'd been to on Broadway, with plush red velvet seats, chandeliers hanging from the ceiling, and a stage large enough for the entire Wakanda royal court.

King T'Chaka is alone at the front of the auditorium, and he turns to see his guards standing with Mars.

"Isn't this magnificent?" he proclaims, and his voice echoes throughout the theater as he walks over to Okoye and Aneka.

"Now do you get it?" Mars continues, stepping closer to Okoye and whispering. "We can't let Tree and them destroy this. We've worked so hard selling the serum. This is where the money went. This is for us."

Okoye furrows her brow as the king approaches them. "But, Mars, PyroBliss makes people burn down places like this. It doesn't make any sense. Don't sell the serum and they won't burn things down."

"Burn what down?" the king asks when he reaches them.

"My king, where is Stella Adams?" Captain Aneka asks.

"She is greeting the reporters and bringing them up here. Apparently, she would like me to make a speech on this stage. Tell me, Mars Cooper, what should I say to the cameras?"

Mars looks at Okoye, then at Aneka, and says to the king, "PyroBliss doesn't make anyone destroy property.

The homes and buildings are casualties or innocent bystanders to something that's supposed to get your mind off things for a little while. PyroBliss is all about seeing the beauty and wonder of one of the most powerful forces in the world. Besides, no one is forcing anybody to take the serum. It's a free society and a free-market economy. I needed some money while I go to school, and NNLB was willing to give me a job. They're taking good care of me."

Mars goes to the other set of elevator doors just as they open, and the rest of her crew walk into the auditorium. They look just as shocked and amused at all the splendor in this place. As Stella had promised, waiters begin to emerge from hidden doors alongside the auditorium.

Okoye steps closer to Captain Aneka and the king. "Do you see what is happening here?" she whispers. "There are no beggars on the streets. There is no visible war with soldiers and tanks. But there is a great big battle happening in Brownsville. My king. Captain. I want to give these kids what was given to me: an opportunity to learn to defend themselves and defend something they believe in. And I understand if you can't support that, but I have to do it, one way or another."

"Okoye, trust your instincts," King T'Chaka says. "I've been to enough places around the world to know when entire countries are being stolen from right under the people's noses without them knowing. This is why I do not want to open up the true Wakanda to the rest of the world. It's clear that Stella wants to push NNLB into Wakanda and she thinks I am a fool. And she has no intentions of giving this building over to the people of Brownsville, or else she would have allowed them to speak at this press conference. My Kimoyo bead has been able to tap into NNLB's databases. Yes, it is true that they had noble yet lofty goals in the beginning, under Ms. Adams's husband's leadership. But it's become clear that Ms. Adams wants more power than her husband had intended. I've seen the documents highlighting her plans of expanding NNLB Industries to other nations in order to take control of their economies and governments under the guise of humanitarian efforts. Okoye, I commend you for taking a stand to help out these children and their beloved community. I support you, Dora Milaje."

"Thank you for understanding, my king," Okoye says, bowing her head in gratitude.

"I stand with you as well," Captain Aneka says. "However, Okoye, you have to be very careful and strategic."

"We've been trained well," Okoye responds. Out of the corner of her eye, she sees Mars and the rest of the crew heading toward one of the hidden side door exits. Okoye's eyes meet Aneka's, and her captain gives her a nod of approval.

"Go!" Aneka says. "There are strange things happening here and all is not as it seems."

The elevator doors open and the reporters and their camera crews start to arrive. Stella is right behind them, and she heads straight for the king. "Are you ready to dazzle the media with your wit and wisdom, Your Highness?"

"Well, Ms. Adams," the king begins. "On second thought, why don't you have someone from Brownsville speak on the people's behalf? Mars Cooper, perhaps? Or one of her friends?"

But as the king says this, Mars is already exiting the theater.

Okoye steals this chance to follow her as the crews set up their cameras. She eases away from the incoming guests as the king and Captain Aneka pretend to do their usual smiling and small talk—their diplomacy.

CHAPTER 13

The side door leads to a narrow, dimly lit hallway where more closed doors line the hall. Most of them have the words *dressing room* written on them. Others simply have a sign that reads PRIVATE. Okoye hears a door slam at the far end of the hall. She quickly makes her way toward the sound of fading footsteps. It's a staircase, and she slowly and quietly steps out onto the first landing and peeks over the railing. Mars and her crew are racing down the stairs.

Within a split second, Okoye leaps over the railing, swings over a banister, and lands on a set of stairs on the floor below. She repeats this several times until she is just one floor above Mars and her friends. Hopefully,

Mars doesn't hear her, and soon Okoye reaches the very last floor, where another door leads out of the stairwell.

The door is about to close, but Okoye leaps again to place her foot right between the door and the doorway before it locks. She quietly opens it, tiptoes out of the stairwell and into what looks like a brightly lit basement warehouse with dozens of large cardboard boxes. At the far end of the floor is a room surrounded by wide windows.

Okoye eases behind boxes and around the many columns and poles in the basement, watching Mars and her friends meet with another set of kids who shake Mars's hand and whisper as if concocting some sort of plan. Okoye can't hear them, but she pulls a Kimoyo bead from her bracelet, places it in her ear, and the sound of their voices is amplified through the bead.

"She wants to expand outside this country," Mars says to the others. "We're heading to Africa soon. That's why she had those people from Wakanda come here."

"Africa is not gonna fall for PyroBliss," a boy says. "They can't even afford it."

"You could say the same thing about Brownsville or Harlem. When the people want PyroBliss, they will find the money," Mars says.

"Then why does Stella only want it in places like Bed-Stuy and Harlem and Africa, where people can't afford it? Why can't we push it in Park Slope or the Upper East Side or even London and Paris?" a girl asks.

"I'm sure Stella has plans to take PyroBliss all over the world. But she gotta start somewhere, right? You know, started from the bottom . . ." Mars laughs and starts to do a dance.

"Sounds like you know a lot about what Stella's plans are. So she's training you to be the next PyroBliss mogul, yes?"

"You're starting to sound like Tree," Mars says. "You can go over there and join them and be homeless with no job. Your choice."

"Mars, is it true they're trying to get rid of Tree?" another voice asks. "I heard that Tree is too much of a liability for what Stella wants to do."

"You talk too much," Mars says, lowering her voice. "And I don't know anything about that."

Okoye discreetly gets closer to the group, tiptoeing behind more boxes and poles until she's close enough to the room with all the windows. Pipes of all sizes line the tall ceilings and the place looks more like a factory than a subbasement. Behind the windows, people in white lab coats stand around tables covered with chemistry sets—beakers, crucibles, and graduated cylinders filled with bubbling and fizzing liquids in all colors. Okoye moves to another pile of boxes to get a better look at what the chemists are doing. She removes a Kimoyo bead from her bracelet and holds it up toward the chemists. The bead vibrates between her fingers, zooming in on the liquids in the graduated cylinders. "They are making PyroBliss!" Okoye exclaims. The bead zooms out to survey the chemist and the lab once more, recording all the various charts and data on the tables and on the walls. She snaps the bead back into her bracelet. "At the very least," she whispers, "this will be proof."

Okoye senses something behind her. She doesn't turn to look. Before a hand even lands on her shoulder, she spins a full one hundred and eighty degrees and grabs a tall, burly man by the collar. It's one of the guards who surrounded the building. He tries to yank Okoye's arm from his collar, but Okoye takes her other hand and pulls both his arms behind him, twisting his wrists until he begs for mercy.

"Who are you?" the man says, barely able to breathe.

But before Okoye answers, several more men rush to the guard's defense, surrounding her while pointing their guns.

"Let go of him and hands up!" one of the guards shouts.

Mars rushes to the scene and stands behind the guards with wide eyes. "You followed me down here?" she asks.

"You are manufacturing PyroBliss in this building," Okoye says.

"Who's this African chick?" one of the guards asks.

"One of Stella's people from Wakanda," Mars says. "Fall back. She's just being nosy."

"Mars, why are you doing this?" Okoye says.

"Don't move!" a guard commands.

Okoye rolls her eyes as if these guards are a mere nuisance. They look so primitive pointing their guns in her direction. So she steps forward and before anyone can even think about pulling a trigger, she kicks a gun out of one of the guards' hands. Okoye becomes like a tornado as she spins, kicks, and punches all five of the guards until they are completely disarmed and lying on the floor, sprawled out over toppled boxes and left whimpering in a corner, begging for mercy.

Mars and her friends watch in awe as the chemists in the nearby room press their faces against the windows, trying to get a glimpse of this warrior woman.

"What was that? Some kind of Wakandan karate?" Mars asks.

"Please, child. Do not insult me or Wakanda or karate," Okoye says. She starts to make her way over to Mars, who is slowly stepping back, but a loud buzzing sound forces Okoye to freeze and duck. Bright red lights flash in the distance and the guards start to scurry away, rushing toward the elevators. The chemists in the room run for the doors leading to the stairwell.

Mars looks around and, as if she's forced to make a decision she doesn't agree with, she finally hurries over to Okoye and says, "You gotta leave now or else you'll never see Wakanda again."

"No, *you* have to get out of here. You have to leave now. Come with me, Mars," Okoye says. "Stella is making you do things you shouldn't be doing, just like PyroBliss."

"Look, Okoye. Would you stop thinking that I'm some kid who can't make decisions for herself?" Mars demands. "You just got here. You don't know what it's like to live here in Brownsville. This ain't Wakanda, where kids don't do anything but go on safaris and hunt for elephant tusks or whatever. We got real problems, and you can't just come up in here and beat people up with your African acrobatics and think you can save the day." Mars points to the other end of the basement, where there's a freight elevator. "Don't press the button or else they'll know you're in there. Just jump over the gate. I've seen you jump that high. The elevator will move as soon as you're on there. Now get out of here!"

Mars takes several steps back before she turns around and runs to the elevators just as the doors open and a bunch of guards rush out to survey the basement.

"She's over there!" someone calls out.

Okoye has no choice but to follow Mars's directions. She runs to the freight elevator, leaps over the gate, and in an instant, the elevator lifts all the way to a top floor. When it stops, Okoye is surprised to see that she's all the way up on the roof of the building, where she can see out over the entire neighborhood of Brownsville, and most of Brooklyn, too. Maybe the skyscrapers in the distance are Manhattan's skyline. She looks around to see more boxes, and in the center of the roof, she notices what she thinks is a landing pad for a helicopter.

The truth settles over her like a heavy downpour during Wakanda's rainy season: Stella and No Nation Left Behind Industries are running an entire operation right in the middle of Brownsville to distribute PyroBliss to the world.

On the far end of the roof is a fire escape ladder that leads down to a dark alleyway. She can escape, but she has to come back for the king and the captain. In minutes, Okoye is racing down the streets of Brownsville, away from the community center and toward Lucinda Tate's office.

CHAPTER 14

Stella's goons will be searching for her, so Okoye has to be very careful not to stand out too much in Brownsville. She's wearing a black dress with heels, and while everything stayed put while she was fighting the guards in the community center, she needs a pair of jeans and a hoodie—something like the outfit she'd worn the other night. Maybe she can borrow something more comfortable to wear from Lucinda. She will ask only after she offers to help Lucinda take back the community center for an even exchange. Okoye had gotten the blessing of her king, and now there is nothing to stop her from responding to Lucinda's call for help.

Okoye walks past other pedestrians, people hanging out on front stoops and corners. She ignores the stares and whispers, but when she hears someone say, "She's one of those NNLB people," she stops and confronts the person.

"What do you know about NNLB?" she asks an older man with a thick, graying beard.

"They're snatching up kids left and right, and paying them lots of money to be their eyes and ears here in Brownsville. We don't want any trouble," the man says.

"I do not work for NNLB. Please tell me. What trouble would you have with NNLB?"

The man looks her up and down and says, "I thought so. You don't look like you'd be that stupid. Are you one of those young reporters?"

Okoye looks around and says, "Yes."

The man looks around as well and then he looks down at Okoye's clothes. "Where's your camera crew? Your phone to record? Your pen and notepad?"

Okoye blinks several times as she tries to find an answer for the old man. She remembers her phone and quickly pulls it out. She presses the record button and holds the phone up to the man.

He steps closer to Okoye and whispers, "I'll tell you this much: They took over that building that Councilwoman Tate worked so hard to renovate. They plan on taking over everything in Brownsville, and when that happens, where are we gonna go? Huh? Some of us already got pushed out of all the other neighborhoods in Brooklyn, and some of us been here since forever. But none of that will matter now. They're already moving forward with their plans. Councilwoman Tate was supposed to get all these people rallying around that building and helping this community out, but those people over at NNLB have too much power. Plus, they got our kids pushing that PyroBliss. It's not a conspiracy theory. It's fact."

The man starts to walk away, but Okoye goes after him. "Who is stopping this from happening? Why isn't anybody fighting back?"

The man turns to look Okoye in the eye, but then he looks past her as if she isn't even there. "We don't even know what we're fighting. It feels like whatever it is that's keeping us down and out is coming from the sky, the ground, from around dark corners. We vote, we march, we take pictures, we write letters and articles. Nothing. It's like whoever's out there listening has purposely turned away. We old folks leave it up to the young people. Half of us got jobs to get to, and the other half is bone-tired. Make sure you put that in your little school newspaper or whoever you work for." Then he points his chin toward something behind her and says, "Just ask those kids taking that Bliss. They'll tell you what's really going on around here."

Okoye turns back to see billowing smoke rising from a building in the distance. She races in the direction of the smoke, heels and all, and as she gets closer and closer, her heart begins to feel as if it's sinking into the unknown depths of her soul. It's Lucinda Tate's office. The councilwoman's sign she'd seen a few days ago when she was coming out of the subway is going up in flames. A small group of people stand in front of the burning building, some watching in horror, others watching in awe as if they are witnessing beautiful fireworks.

"Lucinda!" Okoye calls out, thinking that Lucinda might be trapped inside. She rushes toward the building, but the flames are too hot and the smoke is too thick.

"No, get back!" someone calls out from behind her. Before she can even turn to see where the voice is coming from, Okoye is knocked off her feet, falls to the concrete ground, and rolls away from the burning building. Someone's arm is wrapped around her tight, and in one fell swoop, she maneuvers her body so that she has subdued the person in a choke hold.

"Ow, let go!" a girl says. It's Tree, and Okoye is surprised by how strong she is. Okoye immediately lets go of her and rises to her feet while also helping Tree up.

A loud explosion roars through the air and a gush

of hot wind feels like flames against Okoye's skin. The building has completely collapsed, and the small group of pedestrians has now become a large crowd. Sirens go off in the distance. The voices are a mix of joy and frustration, elation and rage.

"Y'all burned down the councilwoman's office?"

"Look at all those dope colors!"

"That building was falling apart anyway."

"Who's gonna fight for us now?"

The voices fade as Okoye focuses her attention on the person who pulled her from the impending explosion. Tree wipes herself down and rubs her neck. "You didn't have to do that. I was just helping you."

Okoye wants to tell her that never in all her years as a Dora Milaje in training has anyone ever saved *her*. Other Dora have helped her get out of trouble on a few occasions, but this teen girl in a broken neighborhood in New York City may have saved her life. Okoye is left speechless.

"You could start with *thank you*," Tree says. "And now you owe me."

"I appreciate it," Okoye says. "But I thought Lucinda Tate was in there."

"The buildings in Brownsville are burning, but not the people of Brownsville, thank goodness."

"Where is she? I was coming to see her."

"Who knows? Last I heard was that she didn't want to be anywhere near the community center while NNLB was having their press conference. They basically forced her to give up that building because they thought this would happen to it. All she wanted was some money to get the programs running, but they wanted to be the ones running things."

Okoye notices a group of kids who look to be about Tree's age watching the flames as if they are completely under their spell. "How does PyroBliss make them do this?" Okoye asks.

Tree starts to answer, but a boy walks up to her and says, "I only have a twenty."

"I'm out of the game, bro," Tree says.

"What you mean you out the game? I thought you were running the game. Mars isn't around, so who else can we get it from?" the boy says.

"Let's get out of here," Tree mumbles to Okoye as she walks away from the boy.

"Hey, Tree! Where did everybody else get theirs from?"

"We're all out! It's over. Look what it's doing to our homes," Tree says, although Okoye can see the shape of a serum bottle stashed in her pocket.

As soon as they're away from the flames and the fire trucks rushing toward the scene with their sirens blaring, Okoye asks, "How do they do that? I don't see any gasoline or igniters. What did they do to set a big building on fire like that?"

"The same way you leapt over them cars the other night," Tree says. "Magic."

"What I do is not magic. It is from hard work and lots of training. But PyroBliss is a magical potion?"

"It's a serum." Tree digs into her pocket and pulls out the tiny bottle. "It's amazing how something so small can cause so much damage. Science can do a lot of good, but it can do a lot of bad things, too. You can have this, but don't be stupid with it."

"Of course not. Thank you," Okoye says, pocketing the serum and making a mental note to examine its contents later. "If it makes people do evil things, then I don't want any of it. Besides, taking drugs is against our code of conduct."

"Code of conduct for who? Wakanda? Yeah, well, we have laws here and everybody breaks them," Tree says. "Look, Okoye. Bliss is not evil. It just gives you powers, that's all. It's pyrokinesis—the ability to control fire with your mind. But the problem is when people want more of that blissful feeling, they get more powers. And once the flames get big and out of control, they can't rein in that power."

Okoye looks back at the people in the crowd, who

have all broken up and gone in different directions as the firefighters rush to put out the flames in the building. Then she sees a smaller group of kids gathered around a trash can. They stare at it as if waiting for it to do something. Then, in a few seconds, the top of the trash can combusts into flames.

"So they are not starting these fires on purpose?"

"No. It starts with just a thought. It focuses all your energy into something that will ignite a flame. It's like PyroBliss is the lighter and our thoughts are gasoline. The fire moves and moves depending on what you tell it to do. The colors are so bright and intense that you can't help but stare at it, and the more you stare, the bigger the flame gets. But by the time that happens, the power wears off and the flame goes back to controlling its own self."

"So you want more of that feeling, that power, and you take more PyroBliss. And more, and more. You end up wanting to control bigger and bigger flames. Hence the buildings," Okoye says, watching the kids manipulate a flame over the trash can. The flame morphs into different shapes—a flower, an ocean wave, then a whirling tornado. Then the flame moves down to the ground until the entire trash can becomes dazzling fireworks. They step back, laughing and cheering.

"Does that look evil to you?" Tree asks.

"No. I don't want to admit it, but it's beautiful," Okoye says. "But don't they see what it does to their homes? Do they not feel any regret?"

"It starts out as fun and innocent, but it gets out of control. They can't stop. They think that the thrill of seeing those magical flames is much more fun than trying to stop all the changes that are happening around here. Look at my neighborhood! It's about to be completely destroyed! I needed the money, but it's not worth all this destruction."

"Stella Adams and No Nation Left Behind Industries are to blame, not your friends. Not the people who live here."

"Stella didn't give us a choice other than to push PyroBliss out on the streets. It was a job. We made money. And then she added bonuses like an apartment and trips to the city. Worst decision of my life." Tree's eyes are red with rage and regret. They start to tear up, but she sniffs back her cry and turns away from Okoye.

"Mars took over, correct?" Okoye says, wanting to soothe this crying girl. But as a Dora Milaje, she's learned not to let her emotions get the best of her, and she's not sure how to comfort Tree.

"Mars and I are from the same hood, but we have different views of the world," Tree says. They stop at a quiet corner near a boarded-up row house. "Look,

Okoye. We know that you're a bodyguard to the king of Wakanda and we know you don't like Stella and how she's trying to get the king to invite her there. We've seen her do that with the presidents of small, poor countries. But you're still an outsider. You don't know how deep all of this is, and you can't just come up in here and think you can save us so easily. But we still need your help."

"You are right, Tree Foster," Okoye says. "I want to help. But I was not trying to be a super hero. I am part of the Dora Milaje and we are the royal guard."

"We saw how you jumped over those cars, kicking butt and taking names. Show us how to do that," Tree says, stepping back and trying to mimic some of Okoye's combat moves. "Show us how to form an army."

"But this is much more than a fight with spears and kicks. You are battling something you cannot see or punch," Okoye says.

"Yeah, but we can definitely kick Stella Adams's butt. We can take her down and she'll back away when she realizes that we're not gonna let her get away with any of this," Tree says. "What about your king and that other girl? Are they down with all of this?"

"Captain Aneka? I have my king and my captain's blessing to help you. Now, where are the others? And we must find Lucinda Tate."

Tree motions for her to follow her down a street with more row houses. Some are well maintained with flower boxes and bars on the windows. Others are boarded up and a few have FOR SALE signs on the tiny lawns. A few guys hang out on the stoop and nod at Tree while eyeing Okoye suspiciously.

Tree stops at one of those houses and a guy wearing a T-shirt, a gold chain, and jeans walks up to her. "This the lady you were talking about? She looks like one of NNLB's people," he says.

"I am not! I am part of the Wakandan royal guard," Okoye says, and she pulls off her wig to reveal her Dora Milaje tattoo.

"That's fire right there," the boy says, pointing to her head tattoo.

"I am not on fire," Okoye says.

Tree shakes her head and says, "It means that he likes your head tattoo."

The boy laughs. "Yo, she really is some type of warrior! A'ight. Come through." He motions for Tree and Okoye to follow him up the stoop steps and into his house.

"This is my cousin Caleb," Tree says. "Last summer, I stayed with my uncle and aunt to finish up my last year of high school since my parents had already moved out of the city. That's the story with a lot of us these days. More than half the kids I grew up with have already moved out."

They walk into a living room, where most of the crew who had been with them in the apartment are sitting on couches, at tables, or standing against walls.

"Where are your parents?" Okoye asks. "Why aren't your families coming for you? Are they not worried about you?"

Some of them shake their heads. Tree exhales and says, "Most of them are working long hours. My auntie says that this is better than hanging out on some corner. Here it's safe. There's food in the fridge, and if they need to spend the night, there's enough room. Our parents know where we are. We look out for each other here. We figure that if we stick together, there's less of a chance that either one of us will be out there taking or selling that PyroBliss. If one of us gets caught up in that mess, there's always a home to come back to so we can fix what's been broken."

"Then why did you sell PyroBliss to people in your community in the first place?" Okoye asks, scanning all the faces in the room.

"Because it's a business just like every other business," someone says. "Capitalism."

Tree nods and says, "It was a job just like any other job, but with way more money and more perks, like those fancy apartments."

One of the kids offers Okoye a seat and a can of soda, but she refuses. "And what about the community center? How was it supposed to help?" Okoye asks.

"Lucinda called it a safe space. It was a 'No PyroBliss Zone' and everybody in the community knew not to mess with it."

"But if PyroBliss makes you do things you are not aware of, what's to stop people from setting a brand-new building on fire?"

"Code. That's the thing Stella and her goons don't understand about us. Lucinda used her own money to renovate that building for the community," Tree says. "We offered her more money to help her pay for furniture and get some of the programs up and running. But she refused to take it when she found out it came from selling PyroBliss. All these politicians promised to furnish the center and stock it with all this equipment for a music studio and a computer lab, but they never came through. Stella saw that as a sign that Lucinda wouldn't be able to keep it up. So Lucinda took money directly from NNLB investors who believe in their mission and don't know what's really going on. At least that money was somewhat legit. The bad thing is that money came with strings attached—Stella Adams, who claims to be helping her fellow New Yorkers."

Caleb interjects: "This is basic information. If you're from Africa, you should know that this is how colonization works. They come to take over, we fight for our freedom, we try to do what they did, we fail, and then they come back to take over in different ways."

"Yes, I've been briefed. Gentrification is the new colonization," Okoye says. "So you want to take back Brownsville?"

"Yes!" Tree says. "I mean, we weren't always on the same page. Once that Bliss wears off, you start to see the damage you've done. Either you feel terrible and try hard to stop, or you feel helpless and keep going because you think the damage has already been done."

"Yeah," Caleb says. "What did it for me was a big rainstorm we had one night. Can't start a fire in the rain, right? The makers of PyroBliss didn't think of that. It was like that cool, hard rain coming down put some sense into us. A bunch of us were on the streets just letting the rain wash away everything that we'd done up until that point. The thunder was loud, the sky was dark, flashes of lightning. . . . It was like we got a second chance. Not all of us, but enough of us. And all I wanted to do after that night was to go home and make it all stop."

"The next day," Tree adds, "we walked around Brownsville as if we were given a new set of eyes. The corner store where we used to walk to when we were little? Gone. Our favorite sneaker spot where we'd get the latest joints? Gone. Gloria's Kitchen that made the best Jamaican beef patties? That bomb lo mein and Szechuan over at Kim's? Where we would get our nails and hair done? Gone. Gone. Gone."

Everyone in the room either sighs or murmurs under their breath—all in agreement with Tree.

A boy steps forward and says, "Not all of us fell for this whole PyroBliss thing in the first place, but we were outnumbered. It took us a while to realize that we want this stuff out of Brownsville. What I hate about the news is that just because a few of us are doing something, they make it look like we're all out here doing it."

Then they break out into exasperated murmurs about how Okoye is slow to understand what is really happening in their community.

"How is she going to help if we have to school her on kindergarten-level politics? She should know this already," another girl says.

"I thought you said she was a warrior. She should

know the difference between good and evil," another kid says.

"Ey!" Okoye interrupts the chatter. "You tell me that I don't know how things work here, so I have to ask questions. Yes, politics is politics all over the globe, but the rules are different in each place."

Everyone is quiet. Then Tree steps closer to Okoye and says, "We've already been helping ourselves. Councilwoman Tate and so many others have been trying to keep Stella and NNLB out of our neighborhood for a long time. But they have bigger weapons. They have more money and more power. It's like Wakanda versus the world. So here, it's Brownsville versus everybody else."

Okoye takes in each of their faces. They all look as if they could be from Wakanda. She is familiar with the history of Black people in America, how they'd been stolen or sold to European enslavers, placed onto ships, and faced brutal conditions in the New World. She's aware of their fight for freedom and equality. She is in awe of how they wear their clothes, with such style and creativity in ways that are very much like the teens her age in Wakanda. Even as she considers their words, they joke among themselves, laughing in the midst of so much confusion and turmoil. There is hope in their eyes and strength in their souls, much like the people of Wakanda. But they have no wise leader, no heart-shaped herb, no Dora Milaje, and certainly no Black Panther. The very least she can do, with the king's blessing, is give them a fighting chance to win back their neighborhood.

"People of Brownsville," Okoye says. "We will fight for what we believe in. We will fight for what is right and fair!"

They don't cheer. They don't break out in a song and dance. They simply watch her suspiciously. So she will have to prove to them who she is and what she is made of.

But someone bursts through the front door, runs into the living room panting, and says, "The NNLB guards are on the block!"

Okoye immediately rushes out of the house to see a black SUV coming down the street. "Don't leave this house," she says.

She is ready to attack if needed. She is ready to defend herself if they attack first. But Captain Aneka opens the car's doors and motions for her to come forward. King T'Chaka steps out as well. So Okoye goes before her king and her captain with her head bowed.

"I am not done yet," Okoye says. "Things have only just begun. Are we in any danger?"

"They cannot do anything to us," King T'Chaka says. "We have diplomatic immunity."

Okoye steps closer to the king. "This place is burning. A woman with evil intentions is taking over. I cannot just leave them here."

"Okoye, you must understand the difference between war and battle," says King T'Chaka. "A war can be made up of many battles. And in between those battles, there is time to rest, to plan, and strategize."

"At ease, warrior," the captain says. "It's time to rest, plan, and strategize."

Okoye inhales, taking in the truth of her king's words. She looks back at Caleb's house and sees Tree looking out of a window. She nods as a way to say that she promises to be back. Tree nods back as if to acknowledge that Okoye has earned her trust. Finally.

CHAPTER 15

Okoye had to be quiet on the drive back. Things had transpired between the king and Stella Adams, but they could not speak about them while in one of Stella's cars with one of her drivers. King T'Chaka's face was expressionless. Captain Aneka glanced over at her several times. Thankfully, Okoye can always read the emotions of her captain. Her face lets Okoye know that she mustn't worry. Things were taken care of, but Okoye has to be more careful.

Back at the hotel, they all finally exhale as they take the elevator up to their rooms before dinner. King T'Chaka stops Okoye and says, "In times like this, diplomacy is my greatest weapon. It is my job as king of Wakanda to keep the peace between nations, but if negotiations and diplomacy fail us, we will always defend ourselves. Remember that, Okoye, even as you defend the good people of Brownsville."

"Yes, my king," Okoye says, bowing her head.

In their room, Aneka lays out all the events that transpired after Okoye had disappeared into the stairwell. "The show had to go on, of course," she says.

"Of course," Okoye repeats. "So there were more reporters coming in?"

"Not too many, but there were enough people for Stella to ignore the alarms and the commotion among the guards and pretend that everything was going smoothly. Everything was being filmed, after all. She could not let people think that she didn't have control over that little part of Brownsville, especially with all the chaos happening outside," Aneka says.

"She knew it was me, eh? So what was her response to you and the king?" Okoye asks.

"There was no time to respond. The guests heard the explosion outside and saw the flames out of the tall windows. They were rushing out of the community center to get to the scene, but Stella stopped them, telling them that it's too dangerous out there," the captain says. "She made it seem as if the people of Brownsville were doing this without mention of her role in bringing PyroBliss. Was anyone hurt?"

"No. But Lucinda Tate's office is completely destroyed. Maybe that was Stella's actual plan: to have the reporters witness exactly how bad Brownsville is. She went on to explain, of course, that they would not burn down the community center."

"Ah, yes. We did see a presentation on that before the fires started. There was a slide show on how the architects made the entire building fireproof."

"Fireproof?" Okoye says. "That explains it, Captain. Stella Adams is manufacturing PyroBliss in the basement of that building."

Captain Aneka is quiet for a long moment before she says, "You've got your war cut out for you, Okoye, and I will be by your side."

"Thank you, my captain," Okoye says.

Once her captain is fast asleep, Okoye steps into the bathroom. She removes a Kimoyo bead from her bracelet and whispers, "What is PyroBliss?"

Articles, news reports, data, and overall online chatter are compiled and uploaded into the Kimoyo bead, and its melodic, all-knowing voice relays to Okoye:

> *Known to be a happy serum created to allow its user to have*
> *an immersive experience with any of the four elements found*
> *in the natural world: fire, earth, water, and air. First invented*
> *by Dr. Lucas Adams, award-winning chemist and younger*

brother to philanthropist, socialite, real-estate investor, and founder of No Nation Left Behind Industries, Stella Adams, PyroBliss serum gives its user pyrokinetic powers while in a chemically induced euphoric state. First trials of the serum were within controlled environments where users could safely experiment with large objects such as brick walls. However, with the sudden, untimely death of Dr. Lucas Adams, Stella Adams took control of the patent and publicly stated that PyroBliss would be discontinued. But recent speculation claims that PyroBliss serum is being sold on the black market in poor neighborhoods across America. Yet no ties linking PyroBliss to NNLB have ever been confirmed.

Okoye pulls out another bead and holds it in her palm as a hologram extends out from it. The bead had hacked into recent video footage in the lab. Stella Adams walks into the lab, where the chemists surround her. She stands in front of a table that holds several graduated cylinders full of red liquid.

"The serum that is for me, and only me, should be red, like hot sauce. Add a little spicy kick to it just for fun. And I don't want to get hooked on it, so take that chemical down several notches," she says.

"Why don't you try it now?" one of the chemists says. "We can test it out to make sure the pyrokinetic abilities kick in at just the right time."

A dollhouse inside a thick glass box sits at the other end of the lab. Stella is handed a small bottle of serum, and she tosses it back before walking over to the glass box. "What should I be focusing on, the box or the dollhouse?"

"By all means, Ms. Adams, we don't want to burn this whole building down."

"It can't and it won't." She becomes still and focused. In seconds, sparks start to fly around the dollhouse. Soon flames start to dance inside the glass box. The fire grows and grows and grows. "I like it," Stella says. "But why don't we upgrade? Dollhouses are for amateurs. Buildings and houses are for the powerless and poor. Let's add some more spice and make it work on, say, people."

The chemist looks around at all the scientists in the room. "We can . . . we can make that happen," he says, his voice trembling.

The hologram retreats back into the bead and something heavy settles in Okoye's belly. She inhales deeply, knowing that a war is brewing in Brownsville.

There are only three days before Okoye, Captain Aneka, and King T'Chaka have to leave New York City to return home to Wakanda. The king is slowly distancing himself from Stella Adams and NNLB, despite the fact that they have paid for his trip. He devotes these last few days to helping Okoye devise a plan for the people of Brownsville.

When they're seated in the hotel's restaurant for breakfast, even a casual meal feels like an important meeting when it comes to King T'Chaka. "Dora Milaje," he begins as he sips his coffee, "an important part of being a citizen of the world is to cultivate deep empathy for people of all nations."

"With all due respect, my king," Okoye interrupts. "Empathy is not action. What do we do beyond feeling sorry for a people who are suffering?"

Captain Aneka clears her throat while glaring at Okoye. Maybe Okoye has overstepped her boundaries by questioning the king like this.

"You are correct, Okoye," the king says. "However, I am leader of Wakanda, not leader of the planet." He lowers his voice. "Even with all the Vibranium we possess, we are still vulnerable. Remember, Europe is much smaller than the entire continent of Africa, but the Europeans managed to colonize the world. And Great Britain is the size of only one African nation, yet they were able to spread their empire throughout the globe. Their sun still has not set. We are small fishes in a big, wide ocean, Okoye. Yes, we may be able to help other nations, but greed is our biggest enemy. Nations will come together to take Vibranium away from us. They will not want to share and we will be left with nothing. Even if it is written in the stars that the Black Panther will rise and we will not be defeated, I am not willing to go to war with the world."

"And where does Brownsville fit into all of this? They do not have Vibranium," Okoye says.

"Correct again. But they do have a community, a village, to fight for. But you can't always be there to fight with them, Okoye. And of course, we cannot share Vibranium with them. What is something valuable that you possess that you can share a little bit of with the people of Brownsville, especially the ones who look up to you with so much admiration in their eyes?"

Okoye glances at Captain Aneka, who is smiling knowingly, as if she's already figured out what the king is trying to convey. Then it dawns on Okoye like morning sunlight. "Those girls in Brownsville—Tree and Mars—would certainly want to train to become Dora Milaje. But they would learn much more than physical battle. They would learn about discipline and strategy; loyalty and truth; justice and peace. They already have the fire in them, although misguided."

"Then maybe, Okoye," Aneka says, "*you* will become *their* captain."

A slight smile spreads across Okoye's face, but the weight of the responsibility of training those young women to do only a fraction of what she can do settles in her belly. Tree and Mars don't have a king or a royal throne to protect, and they certainly don't have anything like Vibranium. But they have their home to save, their people, their memories, and their stories. Indeed, this is something worth fighting for with a few of the skills of the most powerful women warriors on the planet.

King T'Chaka, Captain Aneka, and Okoye take a cab to one of the places where No Nation Left Behind Industries has left their mark on all the broken parts of the city. The king canceled an invitation to get a walking tour of Stella's favorite places. He wanted to see for himself along with the Dora Milaje what damage the NNLB has really done to these places. The driver reveals his lip tattoo to let them know that he is one of Wakanda's special envoys. But he is quiet as he drives his king and the Dora Milaje around the city.

"Ah, Harlem!" King T'Chaka says on the drive along 125th Street. "So much history here, but I can see how some of it is slowly being erased."

"Very much like many of the countries and cities all over Africa," Aneka says.

"Tell me, my king, why is it that wherever there are people like us—people of the sun and earth, the moon and stars—there seems to be so much suffering?" Okoye asks.

"Ah, that is a question for the gods and the ancestors," King T'Chaka says. "Though, with a place like this, it is quite evident that all this suffering and poverty is by design. There are powers that want to keep it this way."

Okoye continues to ponder that question as she watches the people on the streets. "This part of Harlem is even more like Wakanda than Brooklyn," she says to the king and the captain. "One Hundred Twenty-Fifth Street is almost like market day back home the way the vendors peddle their wares and their customers haggle for better prices."

"You are right, Okoye," Aneka says. "Their faces are like our faces. Their walk and talk is like our walk and talk, even though the ground is different here and the twists and turns of their words are less lyrical, but poetic just the same."

But when Okoye looks up at some of the high-rise buildings and shiny department stores, she realizes that pieces of this Harlem are being chipped away by outsiders who claim to be bringing progress for the people's benefit. Progress for colonizers means destroying something old to build something new. But Wakanda is not like that. Her nation is secretly the most tech-nologically advanced in the world, and they did not have to destroy any part of the past in order to achieve greatness, although her beloved nation did not stop this from happening elsewhere. In Wakanda, the old and the new coexist, although not always peacefully. There are minor conflicts, yes, but the ancestors and the unborn are like siblings from the same womb—sometimes they get along, sometimes they don't. Here in this city, the future must destroy the past in order for it to survive, and that is devastating. Entire people and their histo-ries are eradicated in the process. Okoye inhales and says, "These are our brothers and sisters."

"More like cousins," Captain Aneka says.

"No, you are correct, Okoye," the king says. "Broth-ers and sisters but separated at birth."

With each passing day, Okoye feels more and more confident that she has made the right decision to help her distant brothers and sisters in Brownsville. She, Captain Aneka, and the king are not just on a tour of Harlem and other parts of the city, they are seeing the damage that people like Stella and companies like No Nation Left Behind Industries have done to these people—her people.

As they drive farther north in Harlem, more

burned-out and dilapidated buildings become visible. PyroBliss has certainly made its way up here, and Okoye wonders if Stella and NNLB have expanded their operations in Harlem. Fire-truck sirens are the background music to this place, yet there are children outside playing games and having fun. Music blasts out of stereo speakers, and the people look generally happy. This is like many of the war-torn countries in Africa where the people must find a slice of joy in the midst of so much destruction and uncertainty.

They drive up to the Bronx, where the scene is very much the same. The effects of PyroBliss are visible not just in the broken landscape, but in the faces of the young people there. The children still laugh and play amid the rubble, but Okoye can't help but notice the gray clouds that hang over this part of New York City, and in those clouds are the sinister hands of Stella Adams and NNLB Industries. Tree was right. This can't be something that the people do to themselves. There are larger forces at play.

"What if we are able to help everyone?" Okoye asks, nearly pressing her face against the car's window.

"You have a generous and noble heart, Okoye," King T'Chaka says.

Captain Aneka touches her arm and says, "You do know that would require a world war, right?"

Okoye nods, knowing that helping Brownsville would only be the beginning. Word would get out. People would talk. And they would eventually have to help New York City and all the Black people in America. It wouldn't stop there. Wakanda would have to save the world. Even with as much technological power as her nation has, it is still a small country where there is both a royal court, farmers, peasants, and skilled warriors like herself. There would have to be great sacrifices.

"Now do you see?" King T'Chaka says from the front seat as if he'd been reading Okoye's mind.

"Yes, my king. Brownsville will be enough for now," Okoye says, exhaling and sitting back in her seat as they drive back to their hotel.

"Again, Okoye, I give you my blessings. Even while you protect the throne of Wakanda, the Black Panther is always a Kimoyo bead away," the king says, smiling and winking.

Tonight she will return to Brownsville, where she will help the kids organize and fight for what is rightfully theirs.

⌂

"We should be wearing our war tunics," Captain Aneka says after they are dressed and ready to leave. Their Kimoyo beads and spears are always hidden in their sleeves. It's like carrying around a piece of the true Wakanda and the truth of who they are as Dora Milaje wherever they go.

"We are fighting alongside the people of Brownsville. Even if we share the rules of our warrior tactics, it's best if we don't stand out too much," Okoye says. So with sweatpants, hooded sweatshirts, sneakers, and fitted caps, the two members of the Wakandan Dora Milaje leave for Brownsville, ready for this battle on foreign land.

Okoye and Aneka arrive at Caleb's house, where they are greeted by Tree and a few others. But Tree motions them away from the block. They walk down several streets until they reach a nearby playground.

"The walls have ears in Brownsville," Tree says, sitting on the back of a park bench. "I don't know who's snitching for Stella. Notice how my crew got a little smaller."

"Where are the others?" Okoye asks.

"Mars is living it up in those condos," Tree responds. "With Stella, they can get jobs, now even an apartment big enough for their entire family, and she can help them get into a better school. Okoye, we don't have anything to offer them other than hope. What Stella did in taking that building from Lucinda made me lose hope. We *hope* we can get Brownsville back to the way it was, but it wasn't all that great in the first place. We *hope* we can get some jobs, but are they gonna pay us the same as if we work for NNLB?"

"Tree Foster, you won't be able to answer any of those questions if you don't fight for your neighborhood," Okoye says. "Wakanda is a great place, but it required a lot of work to get it there and a lot of work to keep it that way."

"Yeah, but it's not like y'all up there with America or China now," a girl says.

Okoye and Aneka glance at each other. If only they could bring these kids back to Wakanda to see what is possible in the world, and what is possible in an entire country made up of people who look like them. "Those countries are playing by a different set of rules," Captain Aneka says. "There are other games to play and you can make your own rules."

"Well, the name of the game is money," Tree says. "They have most of it, so they make the rules."

"Money is not the answer to everything," Okoye says. "Let me show you something."

Okoye motions for Captain Aneka to join her. They both stand in a combat position.

"Is this what y'all do to hunt lions?" someone asks.

Okoye relaxes from her stance. "I am so sorry that

they do not teach you the truth about Africa in school. We will show you. But remember, this is only the tip of the iceberg, as they say." In a split second, Okoye's spear unfolds from out of the sleeve of her shirt. Then Aneka's spear emerges out of her sleeve. With a flick of both their wrists, their spears elongate. They step back and switch their stances to get ready for combat.

"Whoa!" the kids say.

Okoye and Captain Aneka merely practice their tactics, using only the playful, less harmful methods of defeating each other with their spears. It's a performance and they smile as the kids cheer and root for their favorite, who is Okoye. But Okoye lets Aneka win and the kids ask for a rematch.

As they get ready to start their performative combat again, Okoye senses a shift in the atmosphere. She pauses and turns to see Mars and a large group marching in their direction. Okoye glances at Tree, who is clearly distressed by the sight of Mars and what used to be more than half of their crew.

"Have you and Mars resolved your issues yet?" Okoye asks, knowing that it was only yesterday that she heard Mars declare her allegiance to Stella and NNLB, but they may have been at odds for much longer than that.

Tree shakes her head. "Of course not."

Mars is slightly ahead of the group. She stops right in front of Okoye and says, "What's your deal, Wakanda Warrior?"

"My deal is that you are with Stella Adams and you know that what she is doing here is terrible for your home and your people," Okoye says.

"There's so much you don't understand, Okoye," Mars says.

Tree starts to make her way over to Mars, but Okoye stops her, spotting some turmoil in the distance, near the entrance to the playground. A flame becomes visible and Okoye rushes to help.

"No! Get out of their way!" Tree shouts from behind her.

But Aneka runs to help Okoye, pulling the children out of the way of the approaching flame. A jungle gym with two slides and some swing sets attached is on fire. Most children are running from the flames and babies are crying. Others stand and watch in awe.

"Get away from there!" Tree shouts at the kids as relatives and other grown-ups come to help.

The blue-orange colors dance along the swings and colorful bars of the playground equipment as the kids standing around continue to watch as if the fire is a performance of puppets and they are the puppet masters.

"Make it stop!" Okoye says to the kids. But their eyes

are glazed over and nothing but pure bliss is expressed on their faces as the flames shift into the shapes of trees, then a rainbow, then a unicorn. The kids are collectively manipulating the flames while under the spell of PyroBliss.

"They can't put it out!" Tree says.

Okoye steps closer to each of the kids and watches how their eyes are like empty shells. She passes her hand over their faces, but they don't blink. She touches their shoulders and they don't move.

Tree comes over and pulls one of the kids away, dropping to the ground with him until he forces himself out of her grip and stands, rubbing his eyes as if he's just woken up from a bad dream. Okoye and Aneka do the same with the other kids. Some of them fight their way out of their tight hold; others just simply surrender, allowing themselves to come down from their pyrokinetic high.

Still, the flames continue to rage. Okoye looks around the park for any small bodies of water. Aneka points to a fire hydrant at the edge of the sidewalk outside the park's entrance. It's close enough. With a flick of her wrists, Okoye's spear appears again. She nods at her captain, who immediately understands what she's about to do.

"Who are they, anyway?" a girl asks out loud.

"I heard they're NNLB's people," someone responds.

"Nah, I heard they're from Africa," another person says.

The captain gives Okoye a slight nod. Then they both step back and aim their Vibranium spears toward the fire hydrant. The sound of metal hitting metal fills the street, sparks shoot into the air, and the spears break the nozzle off the fire hydrant with such force that the water blasts across the park and lands over the flames like a geyser.

Nearly the entire playground breaks out into a chorus of cheers as everyone becomes drenched from the makeshift rain shower. Others, frightened by what they have just witnessed, rush out of the park. Tree, Mars, and the rest of the crew stare at the Dora Milaje in awe.

"Now I wanna go back to Africa!" a boy exclaims, and everyone nods in agreement.

"We tried so hard to not let this happen," Tree says. "Now we not only have broken buildings, even the playground is destroyed. I wish you could do this for all the buildings that go up in PyroBliss flames in Brownsville."

The kids look bewildered and their eyes seem to search the playground for a familiar face or a few kind words. Okoye crouches down to be at eye level with them and says, "Everything will be all right. You are safe. Now what are your names?"

"None of your business!" one of the kids says. "Who do you think you are? A super hero?"

Okoye is taken aback. "No. *You* are a super hero. And you, and you . . ." she says, pointing to each of the children before they run toward the gushing, broken hydrant to play in the water.

"Again, for the thousandth time." Tree laughs, stepping closer to the group of kids. "Welcome to Brownsville. They're kids, but they don't trust outsiders coming in to save the day. No matter what you look like."

"I am not the bad guy," Okoye says.

"And they're not going to think you're the good guy either. Now can we have at least one of those spears?" Mars says.

Okoye and Aneka return to the hydrant to collect their spears before onlookers get ahold of them. They stop the makeshift geyser by placing the nozzle over the gushing water and using their hands to tighten it shut. The kids boo them for stopping their fun before returning to other parts of the park to play.

"What are those things made of? Voodoo?" Mars asks.

"They are simply spears. With some practice, you, too, can learn to aim like a Wakandan supermodel bodyguard," Captain Aneka jokes.

In an instant, their spears collapse back into their sleeves.

Mars begins to clap slowly, sarcastically applauding Okoye and Aneka for a job well done. "Congratulations," she says. "You've saved Brownsville with your little javelin trick."

"We put out a fire, that is all," Okoye says. "That was hardly a battle."

"If that's all you two have to offer, then Stella has already won. It's not about PyroBliss or the little and big fires everywhere. It's about money. How are you going to use those fancy spears to bring money into Brownsville? Stella has control of the community center. So now all the money that's about to come into Brownsville will have to go through her. She gets to decide how to spend the money and there is lots of it to go around."

"That's PyroBliss money, Mars," Tree says, stepping closer to Okoye and Aneka. "And it's hurting the people here. I didn't realize how bad it could get. Look how young those kids were taking PyroBliss. And worst of all, our homes are being destroyed one by one. The places we grew up, the memories, the things that kept our families together. They're all burning to the ground! So yes, it is about PyroBliss or else she wouldn't have had us pushing it on the streets."

A kid, who looks to be a few years younger, walks over to tug at Mars's T-shirt. "Lemme get, like, ten bottles of Bliss serum for me and my friends."

"How much you got?" Mars asks.

"No!" Okoye shouts. "That's enough!"

Mars walks toward Okoye as she eyes her from head to toe. "*What* are you, really?" Mars asks.

"We are Dora Milaje. We are more than guards. We are warriors," Okoye says proudly, glancing over at the captain and finally feeling free enough to name herself as she truly is in this foreign place.

"Does Stella know what you're really capable of, what you can do with those spears?" Mars asks.

"She may have to soon find out if she doesn't stop making PyroBliss in the community center. Mars, is there anything in your soul that is letting you know that you are not doing the right thing?"

"Right is relative, Okoye. What's right for me is making sure I can support myself and help support my family, but some people think that it's wrong to do whatever it takes to survive." Mars glances at Tree as she crosses her arms as if she's on the defense. "Why don't you use these super-powers to help us get more money into Brownsville?"

"We have to put out all the fires first," Okoye says.

"I thought so," Mars says, uncrossing her arms and starting to walk away.

"Wait. But we can teach you how to fight for what you want, what you need." Okoye catches everyone's attention.

"What exactly can you teach us?" Tree asks.

"We need to come together to fight against Stella and NNLB," Okoye says.

Mars steps closer to Okoye until she is only a breath away. "Be careful. Stella's got more of everything and she can beat you."

As they walk away from the hydrant and toward the benches, several firefighters venture into the park surveying the half-destroyed playground. They look over at the group and turn away as if the slides and swings are not worth their time.

"They always come when it's too late," Mars says.

"It's like they're waiting for it to all burn down," Tree adds.

"So, Mars, you do care whether or not Brownsville is destroyed?" Okoye asks.

"I mean, if there's no Brownsville, then what's the point of being here anymore?"

"Yeah, but you'll have your fancy apartment and your fat paycheck," Tree says.

Okoye notices the sadness in Mars's face. "Mars, what is it that you want?" she asks.

Mars looks up and around the playground. The few children who'd been playing near the jungle gym have all left. Sirens continue to wail and smoke from some nearby fire makes the sky look even redder and cloudy, but in some other part of the city, it's a clear sunny day. "I don't know how this happened," Mars says, almost whispering. "What did we do?"

Okoye looks around. "There is no sense in dwelling on the past," she says. "Let us move forward, Mars. Now, envision the kind of Brownsville you want to see, the kind of home and community you want to live in."

Mars looks as if she is seeing the playground and Brownsville's skyline for the first time. "What did we do?" she asks again.

CHAPTER 16

"When things are unfair, when things are going wrong and you want to make things right again, what do you do?" Okoye asks all the kids who have gathered in the playground.

Mars had called into the park all the kids who'd been working for Stella Adams. Tree gathered her crew as well. Together, they have about two dozen teenagers who are waiting to hear exactly how they will put an end to PyroBliss destroying their community and Stella Adams trying to take over. They sit on benches and on the sidewalk outside the playground.

"When police kill one of us, or when one of us kills one of us, or when we go to jail for something we didn't do or did do, we protest," Tree says. "We take to the streets and shut everything down."

"Elaborate on these protests," Captain Aneka says.

"Like Dr. King and civil rights," Okoye says.

"Yeah, exactly," Mars says. "We stop everything and march everywhere. We sometimes walk to a courthouse or where the mayor lives and shout with our fists in the air."

"Sometimes it's something like *No justice, no peace*, or *Justice for so-and-so*," Tree adds.

"And what does that do?" Aneka asks.

"Sometimes it gets us justice, sometimes we're making a lot of noise just so it can get on the news and our voices can be heard," Tree says.

"And what about when you want to get rid of something, like PyroBliss?" Okoye asks.

They are quiet for a long moment and look around at one another. "Getting rid of PyroBliss is not as easy as it sounds," Mars says. "We can't just tell people to stop taking it, and if they can't stop taking it, they can't stop setting things on fire. See? There's not a lot of us here in the park. There are other kids out there who are looking for Bliss and want to see big magical flames, and in the process, they end up burning things down. They can't see how much damage they're doing to their community and their future because they're caught up in that Bliss."

"And it's by design, eh?" Okoye says.

"I mean, it's in the name."

"But you can fight whoever is really responsible for all of this. You can fight Stella Adams."

"That's easy for you to say because nobody's coming for Wakanda," Tree says. "I looked it up online. It's a peaceful nation that no one is checking for. Why do y'all need warriors, anyway?"

"Every nation needs protection," the captain says, glancing at Okoye. "No matter how small and seemingly insignificant."

"If it were not for Lucinda Tate, we would not have been here," Okoye adds. "So nobody was checking for Brownsville, either, as you say. But you do need protection."

"Well, who does Wakanda need protection from, anyway?" Mars asks.

Okoye glances at Aneka again. They communicate silently this way. An exchange of looks is permission asked and permission granted without either one of them having to explain further. Captain Aneka nods in approval.

"Stella Adams and No Nation Left Behind Industries had plans to expand into Wakanda. She thinks that it would benefit my people to have several community centers throughout the small country. She was trying to get close to our king in hopes that he would agree. Stella Adams planned to pump lots of money and PyroBliss into Wakanda, and in turn, she would eventually own it," Okoye says, looking firmly into both Tree's and Mars's eyes to ensure that they are hearing and understanding her.

"That's messed up," Tree says. "But how do you stop somebody like that who has so much power? If she wants to take over whole countries, what's to stop her from taking over a whole neighborhood? I mean, look at Harlem and the South Bronx. Those places are full of NNLB community centers and PyroBliss is destroying everything around them."

"Yeah, you see what happened to Harlem?" Mars says. "For every burned-down building, there's a brand-new shinier and taller building in its place."

"How do we protect all these places?" Tree asks. "I mean, what if in my wildest dreams we defeat Stella and NNLB? And then what?"

Okoye inhales and looks up at the billowing smoke above the playground. "That is the age-old question, yes? How do we save ourselves and the world at the same time?"

"Okoye, the answer is simple," Captain Aneka says. "That is the work of super heroes."

"Hmph. Captain Aneka is right," Okoye says. "We are simply guards from a small African nation called Wakanda. We cannot save the world. We can only protect our small corner of it. And hopefully, others will see what we are doing and how we did it, and they will be inspired to do the same in their part of the world."

Tree, Mars, and the other kids look around at one another. "All right," Tree says. "Let's do this. Now where can I get one of them spears?"

"At ease, young warrior," Okoye says. "Who are you? What is your purpose here?"

"What is the purpose of that question?" Tree asks.

Okoye motions for everyone to stand to their feet. She asks them to organize themselves into a circle. "It is clear that you know what you are fighting for. You also know who you are fighting. But do you know what you are fighting with?"

"Like I just asked," Tree says. "If you let us borrow one of them magical spears, we'll be all right. And what's in those things, anyway? Wakandan juju?"

"Juju? No. It's purely science, technology, discipline, and strength. It also requires strategy. But you have to know the rules first, very much like you have to know yourself."

"Yes, who are you?" Aneka questions.

Mars points to her friends, who have all taken

positions around them, watching the dispersing crowd outside the playground. "You already met those two. That's Kendra and Neptune and—"

"No, that's not what we mean," Aneka responds.

"We want to know who you are, not your names," Okoye adds. "You have to know who you are on the inside, in your soul, to know what skills you can bring to the battle. You see, Aneka and I both have this magical spear, as you call it. But we just used it in different ways."

Tree and Mars exchange looks, then they cross their arms as they step closer to Okoye. "You want to know who we really are?" Tree asks. "Then you go first. What's Wakanda really about and what made you decide to become warriors?"

Okoye looks at Captain Aneka, who nods again as a way of giving permission to let these Brownsville kids in on their secret. "We are Dora Milaje," Okoye says. "But Aneka and I are very different, much like you and Mars. I'd always wanted to be a warrior, but I was not always confident that I had what it takes. I was an opinionated child, yes. Loving and loyal. I've always had so much respect for the Wakandan throne. But becoming a Dora Milaje meant that I had to make huge sacrifices. I left my family in the countryside and I had to devote my life to the throne. Everything I do is for the throne. I fight for Wakanda."

"And she was not always a skilled fighter, you know," Captain Aneka adds. "While I am swift and assertive with my spear, Okoye is more calculating and graceful. How we fight is connected to who we are. Now, I didn't always want to be a Dora Milaje, but I received a calling, a duty."

"That is true," Okoye says. "We may have found this life in different ways, but we're fighting for a common goal."

Tree is wringing her hands and keeps looking over at Mars, who gives her a sympathetic look back.

"Are you willing to share whatever it is that is bothering you with everyone here?" Okoye asks.

"Yeah, these are my people. They know my story. The thing is, I never really told it, you know. Maybe through, like, rapping or a short essay for school. But no one ever asked me who I really am and for me to tell my story."

"Go on. We are listening."

"We used to live on that same block as the community center," Tree begins. "It was a nice building where the elevators were clean and as soon as we stepped out of those front doors, the park was there. By the time I was ten, Mama let me go to the park by myself, where there was a playground with lots of kids from the neighborhood. And my school was around the corner and down the block. I could walk to and from school by myself and there'd be a bunch of other kids coming from everywhere.

"We used to put barbecue grills outside and everybody in my building and in the next building would be there. People would even barbecue across the street in the park, so it was like our backyard. Music would be blasting and everybody would be dancing. And we would just be free, you know? Until that day somebody called the cops on us and we had to turn our music down. Then we had to clear out of the park and those No BBQ Allowed signs went up. And so did the rent. Mama's lease was up and she couldn't pay what they were asking. It wasn't just the rent—they wouldn't fix things that broke in our apartment. We would have to wait weeks for a new stove. Almost everybody was complaining about the same thing.

"Then the building was under new management—NNLB. And that's when things really started to change. The first family moved out and they had been there since my mama was a little girl. Then things started falling apart in Brownsville. Why does it have to be that way, huh? Why is it that when we get pushed out, they want to make things cleaner and better? It's like we're the ones they want to clean up."

Everyone gathers around Tree as her eyes begin to well up with tears.

"It's clear," Okoye says. "You want to protect and defend your home. You have a purpose, Tree. That is why you are a leader."

"I didn't really think about what selling all that PyroBliss would do to Brownsville," Tree says. "I knew exactly what she was all about and what they were trying to do, but Stella made a promise. If I could get a nice apartment in one of those brand-new buildings, maybe she'd let me keep it and maybe move in some of my family. She said everyone would get an upgrade. No one would be pushed out. Whoever needed a new stove or a fresh coat of paint would get it. It wasn't supposed to be about destroying what we have here. That's why I stopped selling it."

"You were betrayed," Aneka adds, "And you should be angry."

"And I didn't want to take PyroBliss in the first place," Mars begins. "Then I started to think about it in a different way. You see, I'm a musician and a painter. And when I hear something beautiful, I see colors and shimmering lights. I paint what I hear and play what I paint. That first time I took the serum, the colors and lights were so intense, I just knew that I had to get to my guitar and play something that could capture what I had seen in those flames. I couldn't do it. So I had to take more Bliss serum. I had to see bigger and bigger flames. But each time I set something on fire, the colors got more dull. I was chasing colors. I know how those kids out there feel. They want something that they can never have. It's like wanting Brownsville to become like any fancy part of Manhattan, but it keeps getting more and more broken. It's like we're trying to grab air and all we end up with is an empty hand."

Everyone nods in agreement.

"Mars, you understand what PyroBliss is doing to people's minds," Okoye says. "You already had a plan to destroy it, but your purpose is to cultivate empathy. It is not your fault, therefore, you should not feel guilty. No one should be punished for taking PyroBliss or even selling it. It was all because of lies. The person who is really guilty is the one who created PyroBliss and brought it into this community. And we know who that is. We know who the enemy is. Now it's time to fight with more conviction."

"And discipline," Captain Aneka adds. She gets up and retrieves her spear again, offering it to Mars, who hesitantly takes it and almost drops it, surprised at how light it is.

"What is this thing made of? Iron?" Mars asks.

Okoye knows not to say anything about Vibranium. She's just said enough about Wakanda to let them think that it is indeed a humble African nation. To mention

Vibranium, the heart-shaped herb, and the legacy of the Black Panther would be a major transgression. "Yes" is all Okoye says. Well, Vibranium is a powerful kind of metal so it's not a complete lie.

"You have to hold it with your entire body," Aneka says.

"Can I try?" Tree asks.

But before Mars hands Tree the spear, a loud explosion in the distance causes everyone to jump, except for Okoye and Aneka, who immediately start looking for the source of the explosion.

More smoke billows across the sky. Sirens begin to wail.

"It is as if there is war here," Okoye says. "Listen to me, Tree and Mars. You have a team here who is willing to listen to you. You are equipped to lead but only if you know where you are going. Now that you've shared a bit of your story, you know where your passions lie and where you can best use your skills. Tree, you know what you are protecting. And, Mars, you know what you are preventing."

"Yeah, but what are we supposed to *do*?" Tree asks.

Okoye inhales and glances at her captain, knowing that she can't tell them about Vibranium and how it is what their spear and the Kimoyo beads are made of. She can't reveal Wakanda's powerful secret. So she says,

"Find the source of your power and then you will have all the weapons you need for battle. And it doesn't have to be a spear. Use what you have here."

"But all we have is . . . our minds?" Tree says.

"Yes! Your mind is the most important thing," Okoye says. "That is where your will, discipline, and determination come from. Now, are you ready for battle?" she asks Tree, Mars, and the group.

"Do we have a choice?" Tree asks. "They have guns, we don't. Our *minds* can't stand up to guns."

"You will soon learn that guns are primitive, even if they are deadly. And of course, you always have a choice. Defeat or be defeated," Okoye says.

"We could say the same thing about PyroBliss," Mars says, lowering her voice. "Defeat it or be defeated by it."

Okoye taps her pocket to make sure that the small bottle of serum is still there. "Excuse us for a second," she says as she steps into an alleyway with Aneka, out of sight of the kids. "We have to see this for ourselves," she tells Aneka, who pulls out one of her Kimoyo beads and holds it in front of the serum like a microscope.

Okoye makes sure that no one is peeking over their shoulders as she places a small drop of the serum onto the bead. A small hologram appears over Aneka's hand. Instantly, the serum explodes and becomes a swirling flame contained within the iridescent borders of the hologram. Okoye has to adjust her eyes to make sure that what she is seeing through the Kimoyo bead is correct.

The fire sparkles and dances as if trying to lure Okoye to touch it even though it's just a hologram. Both she and Captain Aneka narrow their eyes to stare at the whirling colors. Fire is blue, orange, and red. But shimmering lavender, iridescent pink, and pale blues make these flames a kaleidoscope of mesmerizing colors. Okoye cannot stop staring at it. This must be what someone who has taken some PyroBliss serum sees. The flames start to change. The hologram zooms closer and closer, and Okoye thinks she sees it become an actual rainbow made of flames. Then it shifts to become round like the sun. The Kimoyo bead has tapped into the chemical makeup of the PyroBliss serum and its effect on the user.

Then, in the blink of an eye, the flames become all of Wakanda. She can see it right there! The palace, the savannah, the mound where the powerful Vibranium lies. Then, within the flames, she sees the rest of the Dora Milaje in their red tunics and spears standing before the Wakandan palace as if anticipating a war. Okoye stares and stares to see what new colors will emerge, what shape the fire will shift into, and what memories it will evoke. The flames become a small bottle of serum, then a Kimoyo bead again, but Okoye doesn't want it to stop. She wants to see more.

Captain Aneka touches Okoye's arm. "The Kimoyo bead has shown us the power of PyroBliss," she whispers.

"The first time you take PyroBliss," Tree says from behind them, "all you see are pretty things and happy thoughts you've got floating around in your mind."

Okoye and Aneka turn back around to see that Tree and the others are much closer than they were before. "But I did not want to burn down buildings," Okoye says.

"No, but don't you want to see it again?"

"It was not so bad." Okoye shrugs, understating the effect PyroBliss had on her, even through the Kimoyo bead. "How was it for you?" she asks Captain Aneka.

"That is indeed powerful," Aneka says. "It is a battle of the minds. Us against the flames."

"And that's why it's so hard to get people to stop," Mars says. "Even when they realize that they're about to destroy property, it's too late."

"They tell us kids we shouldn't play with fire," Tree says. "They tell us not to do drugs, go to school and study hard, get a good job, buy a house, be a good citizen, and everything will be all right. Well, that's what my grandparents did, and my parents. But they couldn't even keep their jobs or their houses. We all thought we would be living in Brownsville for the rest of our lives. But how come they tell us to follow the rules that they get to break?"

"Yeah, did Stella and the people like her have to follow those rules?" Mars asks. "She walks around doing all these press conferences, telling people that she's a native New Yorker and she just wants to make her city great again. Great for who? Look, I didn't mean to get on her side, really. But whatever she got that makes her so great, I wanted a little bit of that for myself, too. You can't blame me for that. Like they say, don't hate the player, hate the game."

"So how do we change the game?" Okoye asks.

"First off, we want NNLB to get out of Brownsville. And we want the kids who are hooked on PyroBliss to get help," Tree says.

Okoye steps onto a bench and looks out at all the new kids who have scattered away from the playground. When they see her, they all return and gather around, ready to hear what she has to say.

"You will show the world the truth!" Okoye shouts. "You will take photographs and videos. You will tell your truths. You will speak up to whoever will listen. You will march in the streets! You will demand NNLB get out of Brownsville! You will shut it all down!"

The small crowd shifts, murmuring. They glance

at Tree and Mars, who are hesitant at first, but then they begin to applaud as everyone follows their lead. Lucinda comes into view and she joins them.

"I think this is exactly the motivation we needed," Lucinda says, smiling over at Okoye. "We had the right idea from the start, but we needed that push. Thank you, Okoye."

"No, thank you, Lucinda," Okoye says.

Soon the kids are a chorus of hope and anticipation. Okoye looks over at her captain, who nods again in approval. She catches a glimpse of Tree and Mars holding hands, and she exhales, knowing that she's brought the divided group together, even though it may be a long journey toward peace and justice.

CHAPTER 17

The next day, back at the hotel, King T'Chaka asks Okoye and Captain Aneka for an update. When they're finished briefing him on the situation in Brownsville, he relays some bad news.

"Stella Adams is petitioning for me to be removed from all NNLB humanitarian missions," King T'Chaka says as the three of them stand in the hotel's lobby.

"Well, that wouldn't be so bad, would it?" Okoye asks.

"It is not good, Okoye," King T'Chaka says. "Wakanda needs NNLB to be part of a global effort to help other nations in need. It has power and reputation on the global stage. They were able to fund our trip to New York City and were promising to fund other trips. NNLB is our cover. Without them, we can't simply go galivanting around the world with the message of peace and hope on Wakanda's dime since we're supposed to be a poor, humble nation. There would be too many questions."

"My king, you know that NNLB is just a front to spread PyroBliss all over the world," Okoye says. "Stella wants to set up shop in Wakanda."

"You know that will never happen in Wakanda, at the very least. As part of my excommunication from NNLB, they have asked us to leave a day sooner than we had planned. They changed our flight to this morning. Stella has sent a car for us."

Okoye glances at Captain Aneka. "We can't leave today," she says. "My king, is there anything you can do? Even if NNLB doesn't get to Wakanda, Stella Adams will still get to other corners of the world, especially the ones like Brownsville. We have promised the people of Brownsville that we will be there to help them fight Stella and NNLB. We cannot abandon them now. If they succeed, they can be an example for the rest of the world. Brownsville is only a small neighborhood in this big city, but maybe they can inspire entire nations. They can do what Wakanda has not been able to do."

King T'Chaka exhales. "I am impressed by your deep compassion for others, Okoye. Captain Aneka, get us on a later flight. But it is important that I remain civil with Stella Adams. I cannot afford to offend my allies, even if they do have ulterior motives. We mustn't let Stella know what we are up to. But we will certainly send NNLB a message through the people of Brownsville."

Okoye inhales and holds her chest out with pride. She doesn't often get compliments such as this from the king, but when she does, she feels herself lifted to great new heights. Captain Aneka is smiling at her, too. There is nothing else to do but to move forward with bravery.

Okoye, Captain Aneka, and King T'Chaka do everything according to the old plan. They gather their things to leave for Brownsville, but when they are ready to leave, Stella is seated on one of the leather couches in the lobby, smiling.

"I've come to give you a proper send-off, Your Highness," she says, getting to her feet when she sees the king.

Okoye is cautious as she eyes all the guards positioned in every corner of the hotel's lobby.

"I appreciate that, Stella," King T'Chaka says, staying cool. "It's unfortunate that you saw fit that I leave early."

Okoye keeps her eyes on Stella because the king has gone off-script. He was not supposed to mention anything that would arouse suspicion.

"Oh, there were no ill intentions, King T'Chaka," Stella says. "I just thought you were eager to get home, that is all."

"Ah, yes. Wakanda. I do miss the small palace and peasants and farmers," the king says with a smirk.

"I would love to visit one day," Stella says. "I'm sure Wakandan hospitality is among the best in the world."

"Among other things," the king says. "I am afraid our car is here and we must be on our way."

Stella extends her arms toward the king for an embrace, but both Okoye and Aneka step in to keep her away. The king has already turned his back on her, leaving Stella to slowly drop her arms. "Be careful out there," she says. "I'm sorry you didn't get to know Brownsville . . . I mean, New York City a little better. So many unspoken rules. You'll have to visit again and learn them all so you can take them back to Wakanda and maybe help bring your people into the twenty-first century. You know, civilization, democracy, capitalism."

The king turns to her slightly and without smiling says, "Ah, yes, these wonderful things that make America so great." With that, he turns his back again and begins to walk away.

"I'm sorry you will miss today's grand opening for the community center," Stella continues, causing King T'Chaka to hesitate near the door. "Since I and NNLB will be taking over now, we are finally ready to open our doors to the community. I've already booked a band and motivational speakers. I was hoping that you'd get to see Tree and Mars perform. They've been so helpful in my efforts to reach the people of Brownsville. The reporters will be back to broadcast the whole affair."

Okoye turns to look at Stella and wonders if she is telling the truth. Either way, they will soon find out.

"Sounds like a wonderful event, indeed," the king says. "We are looking forward to viewing it online when we reach Wakanda."

Okoye glances at Captain Aneka, slightly surprised that the king has fibbed. But Stella's grand opening was not part of her plan. Still, it will work in her favor if cameras and the people of Brownsville are already there. That also means there will be more guards present. Okoye is eager to get to Brownsville to ensure that the kids will be safe.

Once they are in the car, they all exhale.

Okoye slips into the front seat, where she turns to the driver, an older man who eyes her knowingly. Okoye nods; then the man nods. He reaches for his bracelet and pulls out a Kimoyo bead that projects a small hologram displaying his Wakandan identity. The man is a Wakandan spy.

"Thank you, brother," Okoye says. "As I mentioned, please take us to the Brownsville neighborhood in Brooklyn."

Okoye then pulls out her phone to call Tree. "Is it true you're performing for the community center's grand opening?"

"Oh, it's gonna be a show, all right," Tree says. "We're still on. Stella and NNLB have no idea what's about to go down."

CHAPTER 18

Tree and Mars had to get the message out through word of mouth. Lucinda knows some local politicians in the surrounding neighborhoods, so she helped to get the word out even further. No cell phones, emails, or even flyers were used. The protest would happen in front of the NNLB community center. And much to Okoye's delight, it had already started by the time they reached Brownsville.

They are only a few blocks away from the building, and they can't make it past the crowd of protesters blocking the intersection that leads into Brownsville. People are crowded onto the sidewalks and some are sticking their heads out of windows as they shout and chant and raise their fists. Okoye can't make out what they are saying, but they are clearly angry, and she smiles. This part is going according to plan. This is the first step to getting the newspeople to take notice of what is really happening in this community.

But she sees something that was not part of the plan. A line of armed guards is at the edge of the crowd. Stella must've found out. All these guards were not supposed to be here.

"I don't suppose this is what Ms. Adams had in mind for this grand opening," King T'Chaka says.

"It isn't safe, my king," Aneka says, noticing the crowd, too. At this point, it's clear that the guards may not be on their side.

"I should find out what is going on," Okoye says. Without waiting to hear the king's orders, she starts to open the car's door, but someone quickly shuts it in her face. A man appears in the tinted window wearing dark sunglasses, a black hat, and a black uniform. He carries a shield, and Okoye immediately notices the weapons at his sides—a gun and baton.

"Stand back, Dora. It looks like they have it under control," King T'Chaka says.

"But we want Tree and Mars to have control, not the guards," Okoye says. "We want the people to protest."

In the distance, Okoye sees more men in these black uniforms with their shields and weapons, and they start to push the crowd back. There are more shouts of protest. Okoye scans the crowd to see if Tree and Mars are among the protesters, but all she sees are angry and bewildered faces. She is glad that news of the demonstration has gotten out, but she didn't want them to have to put up an actual fight against armed guards.

"My king, I have to make sure it is safe out there. I don't want to leave it up to these men with weapons. They are not on our side," Okoye says. She feels her heart racing in a way that lets her body know that she is ready for combat. She can feel it in her bones that something is not right, and she is on the side of the protesting people. So right now, all these armed guards are the enemy.

"Okoye, I will stay here with the king where he is safe," Aneka says.

"Dora Milaje," the Wakandan driver says, "I am here if you need me. I know this place inside and out. Just say the word."

Okoye starts to unlock the door again, but one of the men bangs on the car's hood, motioning for the driver to proceed.

"What should I do?" the driver says. "He thinks I am one of Stella's employees."

"You are, but you are also one of us," Okoye says. "Don't let your guard down."

The crowd is being pushed aside with shields and batons. Just as the car eases toward the crowd where the men in uniform are forcefully moving the people aside, Okoye opens the door and jumps out. She refuses to sit in the comfort of that car and watch these people get pushed around.

"Hey, you!" someone calls out to her. "You one of Adams's people?"

All eyes are on Okoye. A uniformed man rushes toward her. "Ma'am! Get back in the car. It's dangerous out here."

But Okoye races into the crowd, squeezing herself through the people as they chant, "Stay off our streets, NNLB Industries!"

"Hey, warrior lady!" someone from the crowd shouts. "We thought you were on our side!"

"She is!" someone else shouts. "Let her do her thing."

Okoye reaches the edge of the crowd, where more armed uniformed men are forcing everyone back with their shields and batons. Their weapons are mere toys compared to her Vibranium spear. But Okoye has to decide if her Dora Milaje skills will help her out of this situation. Captain Aneka has trained her well and has already given her blessings. So she braces herself as her mind races and her eyes dart from one guard to the next. She steps back where there is an opening in the crowd large enough for her to spin and kick within the blink of an eye. Okoye quickly extends her spear, and the Vibranium sends an electromagnetic pulse into the air, making contact with the guards' guns in their holsters. The EMPs weaken their knees and make them fall to the ground as if they've been hit with multiple Tasers.

The crowd scatters about in a frenzy of awe and confusion, but Okoye keeps her eyes on a podium and microphone that have been set up in front of the community center for an impromptu press conference. A red, white, and blue banner is draped in front of it along with another banner that reads, *A Tree Grows in Brownsville*.

Then Okoye sees her. She lets out a long, deep sigh of relief when her eyes land on Mars, who is standing near the door. At least that part is going as planned. Stella doesn't know what Mars is about to do. Okoye looks around for Tree and the rest of the crew, who are nowhere in sight.

The guards are becoming more aggressive as the crowd's chants become louder and louder. Just as Okoye is about to join in the chanting, someone grabs her arm. In one quick move, she pulls away and grabs that person's arm. As a Dora Milaje, Okoye has trained to never be grabbed, held, pulled, or pushed by anyone. No matter how tight the grip, she can always pull away and become the one who is grabbing, holding, pulling, or pushing in less than a second.

But it's Captain Aneka. "Excellent, Dora Milaje," she whispers. "But release my arm."

"Why did you grab me like that? You knew how it would end," Okoye says, releasing her grip on Aneka's arm.

"Now that I've gotten your attention, let us go," Aneka says. "The king is with the driver and he is safe. We have to move quickly!"

The crowd begins to chant louder as a beeping sound forces everyone to cover their ears. But Okoye and Aneka follow the source of the sound: the podium. They soon realize that the beeping is feedback from the microphone. Within seconds, Stella comes into view.

Okoye's eyes meet Mars's. They nod at each other, but Okoye has to keep her attention on Stella.

"Settle down now," Stella says into the microphone. "I know that I am not the one you wanted to see here. I know that I am not the leader you've been waiting for. But today was supposed to be the day that we finally open up the doors to this much-needed community center. We can move on with the festivities, but since all of you are out here, we thought we'd bring the party to you."

The crowd boos as Okoye and Captain Aneka keep their eyes on Mars, who will be giving them their cue.

"Ladies and gentlemen of Brownsville, may I present to you the king of Wakanda, King T'Chaka, who will say a few words that I hope will help restore Brownsville's trust in No Nation Left Behind Industries," Stella continues.

The crowd finally quiets down as Okoye shoots Captain Aneka a look. They both knew nothing of this speech, and when King T'Chaka emerges out of the crowd and meets their eyes, it's clear that he is caught by surprise as well. Stella wasn't supposed to know that they would be there. She wasn't supposed to know about this protest.

"Traitor!" someone calls out from the crowd just as King T'Chaka steps onto the podium.

Okoye scans the crowd, but she can't find the source of that accusation.

"Wait, y'all! Let's hear him out!" another voice calls out.

Okoye recognizes it as Tree's voice. But King T'Chaka turns to Okoye and shakes his head. Then he steps down from the podium, just as the crowd's booing and chanting escalates.

"I'm sorry, Ms. Adams," King T'Chaka says over the noise. "I cannot hear my own voice over the people's protests. Why don't I return when I can truly speak for the people and their voices are being heard?"

"King T'Chaka," Stella says with clenched teeth. "I was under the impression that this is what you were here for. My guards spotted you in that car. Whose side are you on, Your Highness?"

"I am on the side of Wakanda," the king says. "I thought you didn't want anything to do with such a small and powerless nation as Wakanda, and I returned here because the people remind me so much of my own people."

As King T'Chaka and Stella are exchanging words, Okoye spots Lucinda Tate making her way out of the crowd and onto the podium.

"Everybody, you heard the king. Let your voices be heard!" Lucinda says into the mic. "The world is watching!"

Tree joins her at the mic. "Loud and Brownsville proud, repeat after me: NNLB, keep Brownsville drug free!"

The crowd erupts into louder chants and raised fists.

A new group of guards rush to the podium, escorting Stella away in an instant, and she disappears through a side door of the community center building.

"Okoye!" Captain Aneka shouts, pointing to Mars.

Okoye spots Mars making her way through the double-door entrance of the community center. Inside, Mars opens a stairwell door at the far end of the rotunda.

"Okoye!" someone calls out. Lucinda rushes toward the double doors. "I know this building. What do you need me to do?"

"Be with your people," Okoye responds. "They need your help."

"You are my people!" Lucinda shouts. "I can help."

Okoye ignores Lucinda's pleas and chases after Mars. When she reaches the stairwell, Mars has already gone into the basement warehouse, where Okoye is relieved to find the door open and Mars standing in the center of the basement waiting for her.

"Well done, Mars," Okoye says. "Now we have to move quickly."

"Stay cool, Wakanda Warrior. Getting down here in the middle of a protest was the hardest part. Now let's get rid of this stuff."

Okoye surveys all the boxes of PyroBliss. She looks at Mars, who is doing the same. The lab at the far end of the basement is empty. "So you want to destroy all these boxes?"

"Yes! As long as PyroBliss is being manufactured here, this building will never truly belong to Lucinda and Brownsville. But we're taking this whole thing down with real fire, not that weird stuff from the PyroBliss serum. I need you to turn off the fire sprinkler system. The valve is next to the lab."

Okoye considers whether she can protect Mars while she tries to destroy the drug that is destroying her community. "When I say run, you run toward me and don't look back," Okoye says. She looks around for an escape route and spots the freight elevator that had taken her out of the basement. She rushes to where the valves are and spots an intricate maze of pipes, knobs, and wires.

Okoye looks over at Mars, who is in the middle of the warehouse basement holding a canister of gasoline in one hand and a lighter in the other. "Hurry!" she whisper-yells at Okoye.

In the same moment, Okoye hears a loud bang coming from the freight elevator. The doors open and out rushes a set of guards with their guns drawn.

Okoye doesn't hesitate to run toward Mars, who is quickly pouring gasoline onto the boxes. Okoye tackles

Mars to the ground so that they're out of the guards' sight.

"Ow! This was not part of the plan!" Mars whispers.

"The guards coming down here was not something you planned either, but there they are. I need you to stay down," Okoye says, and releases her grip.

She gets up from the ground and dodges behind the boxes until she gets a good view of the guards as they search all around looking for her and Mars. Okoye counts down in her head from ten to zero, and then she's off chasing after the guards, who shoot in her direction but miss. As she leaps toward one of them, her Vibranium spear extends out from her sleeve and helps break her fall just as the guards point their guns at her. The spear blocks the bullets and in one forceful kick, Okoye knocks their guns from their hands. Then another guard comes after her, and Okoye swings around, kicking him in the face. A few more spins, a twirl of her spear, and another near-deadly kick forces both the guards into submission, and they lie on the floor holding their bellies and swollen cheeks.

"Teach me how to do that," Mars says from behind her.

"You will need discipline," Okoye replies, barely out of breath. "Lots of discipline."

Okoye and Mars quickly turn around when they hear the elevator doors open and out come Captain Aneka and Tree, who find themselves stepping into a gasoline-soaked warehouse.

"We have to get out of here," Aneka says. "The king is back with the driver, safe."

"I can't light these boxes with everyone down here!" Mars says.

Another set of elevator doors open to reveal Stella Adams surrounded by her guards—they immediately ambush Okoye, Aneka, Mars, and Tree.

"Ha! I've been waiting for you, Okoye," Stella says. "I see you're gathering your little minions to take down my operation. What are they using? Wakandan bows and arrows?"

"More like spears," Okoye says confidently.

Tree shoots her an apprehensive look, and Okoye nods as if to say everything will be all right.

Stella laughs. "It's too bad you are only working with an army of teenage girls," she says.

Okoye's eyes widen and her fists clench, but she tries to keep her cool in order to get more information from Stella. She taps her Kimoyo bead to program the recording feature. The bead is equipped with both a camera and microphone so it will pick up everything happening.

"Lucinda is out there rallying the people of Brownsville against me, making them believe that I am the enemy, when it was me who rebuilt this place from the ground up. And she thinks that she knows this building inside and out," Stella continues. "But I know my product."

"What product is that, Stella? PyroBliss?"

"I see you've been playing African Nancy Drew over here, poking your nose around in other people's business."

"It's our business, too, Stella, 'cause we were selling PyroBliss for you," Mars says. "You made us give it to kids just like us so they can burn their community to the ground to make way for your high-rise condos."

"Oh, good for you, Mars! Well, I wasn't going to call it No Ghetto Left Behind." Stella chuckles. "There are hardly any trees here and in other places like this. That's why 'A Tree Grows in Brownsville' is such a great motto for us. I should thank Lucinda myself. And why were you allowing some dusty African to get in your business? You betrayed me, Mars, after all I've done for you."

Okoye steps closer to Stella, but the guards stop her. She doesn't fight them. Her Kimoyo bead is still recording everything, and she can't risk exposing her warrior prowess. Better to play the victim while the world is watching. "Where is she?" Okoye asks through clenched teeth and with tightened fists.

"You've destroyed my plans, warrior princess. We'll have to move this lab elsewhere. The thing that you foreigners don't understand is that the world is much larger than your little corner in your impoverished country. I have many other cities, new and bigger buildings with state-of-the-art labs!" Stella boasts. Her voice echoes throughout the entire floor. "You should thank me for being so kind to keep you out of harm's way. I know you wanted to see some fireworks down here by burning my precious supply. But we have to get these out of here, and I wouldn't want to leave behind any evidence. And you, my African darlings, are also evidence."

The Dora, Tree, and Mars are forced to walk ahead of the guards to a room where it's dark and the walls are made of steel. As soon as they are in, the guards quickly step out and the doors close. Tree and Mars hold hands, and Okoye and Captain Aneka brace themselves for whatever threat the room might pose.

"What is this place?" Okoye asks.

"The doors are sealed shut," the captain says. "Not even our spears will get us out of here."

"We have to find a way to get out of here without them, then," Okoye says.

Okoye looks at her captain with pleading eyes, as

if begging for her forgiveness. Before Aneka can even say anything, Okoye removes a Kimoyo bead from her bracelet. She taps it to alert the king that she is in distress. Then she pulls another bead, programming it to hack into nearby cell towers. She broadcasts the recording of Stella to phones and screens all over the city.

"Okoye, what are you doing?" Tree asks.

"Now everyone will know the truth," Okoye says.

"What's happening?" Mars shouts.

A loud bang comes from the ceiling. Tree and Mars crouch down and cover their heads. Captain Aneka aims her spear, but Okoye is standing firm as if she is expecting something. She quickly taps her Kimoyo bead to end the live recording. The world doesn't need to see what is about to happen.

More loud bangs, and a long screech. Something is slicing through the steel walls. Tree and Mars start to scream. A sharp, cutting sound across the door lets in air and light and a strange figure appears.

Okoye and Captain Aneka immediately bow in his presence. "Black Panther!" they both say.

"Black Panther?" Tree and Mars repeat.

Guards are approaching the steel room, trying to stop them from leaving. But the Black Panther, along with Okoye and Captain Aneka, fights each one of them off. Before Tree and Mars can blink a second time, all the guards are on the ground and the Black Panther is motioning for them to leave. Stella has been rushed out by another set of guards.

Okoye turns back, relieved to see that the Black Panther is close behind.

CHAPTER 19

A new group of guards reaches them before they figure out how to leave the subbasement. Okoye and Aneka have their Vibranium spears ready for their enemies as the Black Panther leaps over their heads and attacks each of the guards—spinning and kicking, punching and blocking, and launching their weaker bodies into the air. They land on the ground or atop boxes, the wind knocked out of them.

Tree and Mars watch in awe as the Black Panther defeats the guards.

Stella Adams comes into view. She walks slowly toward the Black Panther, unafraid.

The Dora Milaje stand beside the Black Panther,

ready to handle Stella Adams if it comes to that. It should be easy.

But Stella's eyes seem to glow a fiery red, almost like the atmosphere surrounding Brownsville. Something is different about her. So the Dora Milaje get into their fighting stance.

"I tried to be nice and hospitable," Stella says, her voice like an erupting volcano now. "These girls told you to stay out of it."

She is focused on the Black Panther, and before Okoye and the captain figure out what she's up to, the Black Panther's feet are covered in flames. Her powers are further ignited by the gasoline on the floor, and the fire spreads, engulfing the Black Panther.

"Run!" Okoye shouts to Tree and Mars, and they make a dash for the freight elevator.

With fire raging across his suit, the Black Panther leaps into the metal room in order to prevent the flames from spreading, goes back the way he came, and is quickly out of sight.

Fire begins to rage throughout the warehouse floor as boxes of PyroBliss serum go up in flames. Stella is frozen where she stands, her eyes locked on the dancing flames. Okoye is torn between pulling Stella out of her blissful trance or getting herself out of the warehouse.

"Let's go!" Captain Aneka shouts from the edge of the freight elevator.

Okoye uses her spear to leap over the growing flames and in one fell swoop, she grabs Stella, dragging her toward the freight elevator as the fires inch closer and closer. As the elevator ascends, they watch each of the boxes of PyroBliss be destroyed by its own progenitor, annihilated by its own creator.

The freight elevator stops on the ground floor, where a back door leads to the street. As soon as they open it, they are greeted by a cheering crowd and lights from phone cameras. Strangers and kids from Tree and Mars's crew come to embrace them as they rush to get away from the building.

Stella is coming out of her trance, but her goons are not around to help her. The crowd forms a circle around her to stop her from getting away.

A loud explosion in the center of the warehouse basement forces everyone to duck. They reach the sidewalk, where there's a crowd looking up at the community center as smoke escapes from its windows.

"Everybody, step away!" Mars calls out.

"Wait!" someone shouts. Okoye and Tree turn to the crowd to see Caleb running toward them. "Lucinda is still in there! She knew you were in the building, so when she saw the first flames, she ran in after you."

In the same moment, fire trucks can be heard from a few blocks away. "Oh, *this* is when they finally come!" Tree says. "When an NNLB building is about to go up in flames."

Okoye catches a glimpse of Tree—her eyes wide, her mouth wide, her chest heaving in panic. "Tree," she says. "Look at me. I want you to breathe. We are going to help. We are all here to help."

The trucks arrive and the firemen rush out to attach a hose to the nearest hydrant.

"We have to get Lucinda out!" Okoye shouts, and she is about to run into the flaming building, but Tree grabs her arm, forcing her to step back.

"You're not superhuman, Okoye," Tree says. "Remember what you said. Science, not magic. I don't want you to get hurt. I want you to make it back home. Let the firemen finally do their job."

A few other firemen rush into the building. As smoke billows out of windows and through the roof, everyone seems to be holding their breath. Okoye is impatient. Tree is right. She is still human and not immortal. She doesn't want anyone to die on her watch, nor on the Dora Milaje's watch. The Dora are trained in combat but are not prepared to run into burning buildings.

The crowd suddenly gasps as the Black Panther emerges with Lucinda draped over his arms. He sets her down on the ground and before anyone can bombard him with questions, he runs back into the burning building even as the crowd protests.

Okoye knows that he will be fine. It is only his exit strategy.

Ambulances and news vans ease toward the commotion, and reporters and their crew jump out, cameras and microphones in hand as they push through the crowd to get to Stella Adams before the paramedics.

"I'd like to thank the people of Brownsville for their bravery and calling the fire department to save my life!" Stella says into a microphone as she gets to her feet.

"Oh, no you don't!" Tree shouts, and rushes to Stella as the cameras continue to roll. "She was selling a drug called PyroBliss and it was being made in the basement of this building. There's still some left if you put out the fire. She's doing this in cities all over the country and she was about to expand to other countries, too!"

Mars follows behind her, stares into the cameras, and adds, "We were not rioting! We want Stella Adams and No Nation Left Behind Industries out of our neighborhood!"

Okoye steps closer to Tree and whispers, "They know. It's been broadcast all over New York City. Good job."

Tree turns to Okoye, smiles, and gives her a long, tight hug.

The crowd breaks out into boos as Stella is taken into an ambulance. Police arrive but they are heading straight for Tree and Mars. The crowd protests even louder, pointing to Stella Adams.

"Arrest her! She's the real criminal here!" someone shouts. "It's all on camera."

But the police simply escort Stella to the ambulance as other police, detectives, and news reporters question the people in the crowd.

Okoye and Aneka glance at each other, knowing this is their opportunity to slip into the shadows. They can't be seen by the news cameras. They can't have King T'Chaka's name attached to this incident, and they hope that Tree and Mars will not mention the Dora Milaje and the Black Panther. Stella Adams will surely keep quiet or else it would implicate her even further in the creation of another kind of PyroBliss.

Okoye turns back to see Tree looking at her. She gives a weak wave as if she doesn't want Okoye to leave. So Okoye reaches for one of her Kimoyo beads and tosses it to Tree, who catches it and holds it in her hand for a long second before she quickly puts it into her pocket.

"What is this?" Tree asks.

"You can keep it to remember us by," Okoye says. "It's from my country, Wakanda. It is not a good luck charm or some kind of talisman. It is not magic. I want you to know that Wakanda is as real as science."

"And as real as the Black Panther?" Tree whispers.

Okoye smiles. "As real as Brownsville. Brownsville forever!"

Tree repeats much louder, "Brownsville forever!"

Okoye and Captain Aneka disappear through the crowd. If there are stories told about their presence in the Brownsville neighborhood of Brooklyn, they will only be the stuff of legends and myths.

CHAPTER 20

"**I**'ve learned so much about American culture, yes?" King T'Chaka says as they wait for a cab in the hotel's lobby. "Did you know that they often call Wakanda the poorest country in the Eastern Hemisphere?"

"Let them believe their myths," Okoye says.

"Thank you for alerting me, Okoye," the king says. "You were wise not to handle everything on your own."

"Aha! So that is how you knew to find us," Captain Aneka says. "I agree. Good thinking, Okoye."

"But those girls . . ."

"You need not be concerned, my king. Our secret is safe with them."

"I trust your instincts, Okoye," the king says. "I know you are worried and will continue to worry about those brave, strong, and beautiful children. But all is not lost. Brownsville's community center has just acquired a significant angel investor who has endowed an anonymous fund to funnel much-needed monies to the local youth for continued schooling, extracurricular activities, and counseling to help them work through the harmful effects of PyroBliss. The manufacturing of PyroBliss has come to a halt and No Nation Left Behind Industries has been disbanded by their board of trustees. Stella Adams is surrounded by her lawyers and is preparing for a press conference to clean up her image. It'll be some time before detectives and prosecutors gather more evidence against her. Powerful people like that tend to get away with a lot of things in this country. But on the bright side, Lucinda Tutu has been given back ownership of the building as well as the other NNLB properties in New York City. They are in good hands, Okoye."

Okoye swallows hard, trying to stop her eyes from welling up with tears. "Thank you, my king" is all she says, even though she feels like giving him a hug. She cannot. So instead, Okoye stands straight and gives her king a firm nod as a way to show appreciation for his honesty and validation.

Captain Aneka comes over to embrace Okoye. "My sister. I am that much wiser and braver because of your wisdom and bravery. That is what the Dora Milaje is all about. Thank you for introducing me to those children. They have a piece of my heart, too."

In the cab, Okoye scrolls through her phone to see the names of Tree, Mars, and Lucinda in her contacts. She smiles, remembering their faces and voices. Even though she'll have no practical use for the phone in Wakanda, she keeps it so she can remember her time and her new friends in Brownsville. Okoye changes Tree's name to an emoji of a tree because she is so deeply rooted, with branches that spread far and wide. Mars is represented by a sword emoji—determined, strong, and willing to fight for what she believes in. Lucinda's name is changed into a cityscape. Okoye is sure that one day, she will become the mayor, or maybe the president. The world will be a better place with someone like her in a position of leadership. Okoye thumbs through her Kimoyo bracelet, remembering the missing bead, the one she gave to Tree. Anything will be possible for Tree and the children of Brownsville, with her help, of course. With Wakanda's help.

-End-